Wolf's Song

By

V. L. Brown

Disclaimer

This book is a work of fiction. The names, characters, locations and events portrayed in this book are a work of fiction or are used fictitiously. Any similarity to actual events, locales, or real persons, living or dead, is coincidental and not intended by the author.

Notice

This is an adult erotic paranormal romance book with love scenes and mature situations. It is only intended for adult readers over the age of 18.

Acknowledgments

Dedicated: To my son, always follow your dreams, but be smart enough to find a new one, if the first doesn't work out. I love you, and sometimes there aren't enough words.

For my mom, who has never doubted that I could accomplish whatever I set out to do, I just had to set out to do it. To my baby sis that never stopped believing in me. LOL, and for Amber who kept saying. "I need more Aunt Vickie." Thank you all, I love you, always.

I would also like to thank a very special couple, the best Aussies ever and my beta readers. Thank you, Berni, and, George for always being there to push me on, even from another continent. For always helping me struggle through my own doubts. Most of all for your honesty, and of course, for liking my book before it was really a book. I'll have another one soon for you to talk about around the dinner table. Xoxoxo

Cover design by Kelly McClain

It's all I wanted it to be, thank you.

www.kellymcclain.me

Also a very special thank you to C.L. Quinn, her writing inspired me to pick mine back up. Her advice has been invaluable to me. There just aren't enough ways to say thank you.

When a weekend camping trip with friends turns deadly, what's a girl supposed to do? Run, and run fast. All right, Aria was willing to admit maybe that wasn't the best idea, taking off into the woods at night with no idea where she was going. Just stamp stupid on her forehead. Or was she? Waking up to the most gorgeous man on two legs playing nursemaid to her, well . . .

Aria doesn't believe in love at first sight, but how is she supposed to ignore the fact that nothing feels more like home than in his arms?

Wraithe never expected to find himself in a relationship, at least not a lasting one. The timing couldn't be worse, there was so much happening, but in her arms he knew only peace, and a love, to last a lifetime.

Secrets are revealed, bloodlines are born, evil is walking the earth, and war is coming. Now, all of that isn't necessarily bad, but here is the thing . . . that's just the beginning.

Chapter 1

How many days now, three or was it four? Aria just didn't know, her body ached so badly. She had been stumbling around these woods in a mindless daze. Unsure of which way to go as she aimlessly wandered, watching for any sign, the smallest hope of a trail that would lead her from this nightmare. Her body bruised, and bleeding, all she wanted was just to lay down, just for a moment, but something kept pushing her on. Whispering to her that she must find the strength to go on, or face the reality that she would die here, amid all the trees. She was so hungry, desperately pushing the thought of food to the back of her mind, by wondering where she found the energy to push on. Help was out there, she could feel it, knew it like she knew the pain in her body. Pain that was gradually becoming a numbness weighing her body down. It seemed only exhaustion, and desperation were to be her friends.

"God, please." She screamed up to the heavens. "Please help me!" The shadows were getting larger, reaching for each other to become one. The trees so dense that what there was of the sun could barely penetrate them. Night was coming again, and the blackness that would surround her. "Move, Aria, for heaven's sake pick up those feet and move." She raged at herself. Struggling once again to move forward through the thick ferns. She pushed herself away from the tree she had been resting against, willing it to lend her strength.

What she heard next should have sent chills through her body, and the hair at her neck up on end. It couldn't be, could it, she thought to herself, a wolf, oh dear God was she hearing things now, or was this night to be her end?

Gathering her arms tightly around her she began moving faster, struggling to lift her legs. Knowing what little light she had would be gone soon, she had to find cover for the night.

Once again it came, that mournful sound, but from where, which direction, it seemed it came from all around her. The panic riding her helped to propel her faster toward, what? She had no idea where she was going, she only knew she had to move. Was she moving toward the wolf?

Looking ahead she saw what appeared to be a darker spot, hidden within the trees, and foliage. *"Rest."* It brushed against her mind so softly she wondered if it was just her imagination running wild again. Where did this feeling of warmth come from? "Okay, enough, this is no time to lose your ever loving mind, Aria!" She fussed at herself, had her desperation pushed her too far?

Reaching the small opening in the trees, Aria found what appeared to be a very small cave. Just some large rocks that jutted out of the rock face that provided enough cover to protect her from the rain, it always rained at night. Most of the front was surrounded by the giant ferns. Moss, and some type of ivy growing from the rock. She had to drop to her hands, and knees to crawl through two large ferns growing to each side of the recessed opening. It wasn't much, but at least the over hang was enough to protect her, and the stones to the back would offer the comfort of some security. Laying back against the smooth stones, and gathering her knees against her, she did her best to relax. For tonight, maybe, she could find the rest that she needed so badly. Closing her eyes it didn't take long for sleep to find her, her last thought was of the soft whisper that echoed in her mind – *"I come, little one."*

∞

Wraithe had to get out of the cabin, it felt like days since he had been outside, but in truth it had only been twenty four hours. He hated paperwork, and what seemed to be the endless reports he had to write, but, hey, that was the job.

It had been a year now since he, and his team were moved here, to these cabins, in the Cascades, and he had to admit the landscape was beautiful. He had always thought himself more of a beach bum type, but after a year here in these mountains, he couldn't imagine being anywhere else. Everything here seemed to call to him, and he wondered if it was really him, or if it was the beast inside him that found this part of the world so appealing.

Five years, wow, had it really been that long since he, and the members of his Black Ops team had been approached? A request from the higher ups, to participate in the "Wolf Soldier" program. They were also told that due to the nature of the program full disclosure would not be given, until later. Accept inception into the program with what they were told, or opt out, that was it. Being deemed "Top Secret", and by agreeing to be part of the program, they would have to give up all family ties, and connections to the outside world. None of them could ever go home. In all honesty, none of them had been prepared for the real truth of what was being asked of them. Luckily most of them didn't have families, and none of them were married.

In the beginning, it was just being put through some of the most rigorous training any of them had ever done. That was something in itself considering they were Marines. They all had also gone through Seal training for the Black Ops work they would be doing. The new constant training, along with what they were told, were medical enhancements, steroids, they thought. Each of them became even more, heavily muscled, leaner, faster, and built for stamina. Six months later it all changed, and none of them would ever be the same.

Moved into individual cells for safety. Another phase of the training was to begin, and they were informed the truth about what was happening. What they would become if the experiment were successful, wolves, shape-shifters. Shock, well that word didn't even come close to describing what each of them felt. Denial, disbelief, and okay, who is the prankster? Had to be a joke, right? Not!

Stiffening, Wraithe could feel his beast rising, taking deep breaths to calm the animal, but this time it only made it worse. It wanted out badly. Raising his nose to the scents around him he wondered if there was something dangerous lurking in the shadows. Normally his beast only rose when it sensed something was wrong, otherwise only when it was called. There was nothing in the air that he could pick up to explain why his wolf was trying to get out. Turning his thoughts inward he asked. "Hey buddy, calm down." He pictured himself soothing the wolf. Thing was, his wolf didn't seem stressed. Rolling to his back like he wanted a belly scratch.

His muscles were tightening, a sure sign he was losing this battle. "Whoa there fella, easy, what's wrong?" The wolf seemed excited, more playful than the intense feelings, Wraithe was experiencing. Before he knew what was going on, a growl escaped from deep inside that sounded a lot like *"mate."* What? What's going on, mate, did the wolf need sex? It couldn't be, he had taken care of that just a few weeks ago. Another side to his teams' new genetics, sex, and lots of it.

Panting, he was panting hard, feeling himself being pulled down inside. He had never experienced this from the animal before, strong, he was so strong. Relaxing he let the beast rise, it seemed the only way to find out what was happening. Learning a long time ago that the more you relaxed during the shift, the less painful it became, so he let his wolf have its way. Every muscle, and bone in his body began to break, stretch, and change, with hair erupting from every inch of his skin. Wait! Looking down, he watched as his fingers lengthened, and sharp talon shaped claws pierced outward from the tips of his fingers, growing long, and lethal. What the hell was happening, this wasn't right! Black hair he was used to, but instead of falling to all fours, and turning into his sleek wolf's form, his body grew upward. His snout pushed forward into a huge muzzle, his fangs bursting forth from his gums.

Running, now he was running, and fast, faster than, Wraithe could even begin to understand. His wolf was fast, but this, this was something he couldn't begin to comprehend as the ground, and surrounding trees flew by, blurring in his peripheral vision. Racing through the forest, his beast tore through what seemed miles of forest in only minutes.

"Mate here, hiding, resting, hurt." Wraithe couldn't believe what the beast was saying, while it slowed, and sniffed the air, moving with ease through the heavy greenery, he asked. "What do you mean, mate?" Entering a small clearing, the rock face in front of

him was covered in dark green moss with large ferns surrounding what looked like a small opening at the base of the mountain rock face. Moving toward it the beast didn't answer, but lowered his hand, and reached out to gently pull back the leaves that hid the small form of a sleeping woman. She was filthy, and bruised, small scratches, and dried blood marring her small delicate features. How had she gotten here, Wraithe wondered, what had happened to her?

Quietly not wanting to disturb her, the beast slowly kneeled, and if Wraithe hadn't heard it, he wouldn't have believed it? "Did you just purr?" Soft and rolling, Wraithe knew it was a form of growling, but it really only came out as a loud purr. "She is hurt, there is blood, let me out so I can help her." He spoke, softly to his beast, but the big guy just snorted, then threw the thought back at him *"must carry back den, safety, then make hurt go away."* Wraithe simply could not believe this, even the link between these two versions of his wolf were different. Where his four legged friend sent more images, to communicate with, Wraithe, this version actually used words. Basic, simplistic, yes, but they were words! The thing, talked!

Five years he had carried this beast inside him, and not once, not one fucking time had he ever felt a difference, another side to him. Shit, were there two now? Recoiling at the thought, Wraithe didn't even want to go there, talking to, and controlling one was bad enough, and now there were two, two!

Easing down, and gently sliding his long arms under the small woman the beast carefully raised her, *"so small, my little mate."* Pulling her close, tucking her easily against his much larger body, he nuzzled her neck, breathing deeply of her beautiful scent. His only need now was to protect her, at all costs. Quietly moving back the way he came, he picked up speed so he could get her back to the safety of the den.

He had sensed the stranger in the woods, watching, but he felt no danger from the man, only peace. A soft whisper echoing through his mind as he began to move quickly away. "Welcome brother." And then the voice, and stranger were gone.

∞

Wraithe was still reeling when they made it halfway back to the cabins. Replaying everything in his head that had happened, and realizing that as strange as it was, nothing could be done now. He had to get himself wrapped around the situation, and deal with it. By making that decision he came to another realization. The more he looked down at the small woman pressed firmly against the beast's chest, the more protective he felt of her, and he simply couldn't grasp why. Maybe it was just his need to find out what had happened to her, to see to it that she was well, and safe.

He also knew that explaining this to his men was going to be interesting. Most all of them, especially the twins, took this change to shape shifting pretty well, but his second, Reaper, that was a different story. Reaper felt that full discloser should have been given before their genetics were altered, and although he understood why Control hadn't told them everything, he had wanted the choice. Still he had stood by the team, and remained one of the strongest of them all, but he also had withdrawn. Rarely speaking anymore unless it was necessary, and even then it was concise, and to the point. Wraithe wondered if this would send his friend over the edge.

Was this something that would happen to all of them, or just, Wraithe, and why now did this version of his beast show itself? It couldn't be just the woman, they had all been on missions where women, and children, had been involved. The beast hadn't risen like this, so again, why now?

Pulled from his thoughts because the slight weight in his arms became more noticeable, Wraithe realized that they were almost back, and the beast was letting go allowing him to rise back to the surface. This beast had quickly, and seamlessly, just disappeared. He even had on the same clothes, okay, that really was different.

She was filthy, and hurt, but looking past the grime she was coated in, Wraithe could see the beauty of the small woman he held tightly against his chest. Scratches, and bruising around her face didn't diminish the soft shapes of her eyes, and nose. The fullness of her lips that made a man want to kiss them.

Wrapped tightly in his thoughts, he didn't hear the twins, until they were almost on him. Both in their wolf forms, in from running the perimeter. They were, Native American from the Sioux tribe, and the twins were something to behold. In their wolf forms, both were a sleek deep gray, so dark it appeared almost blue. There was only a slight difference between them when in wolf form, ones ears tipped in black the other in white. Snows Song, and, Winterhawk, the two were inseparable, and in wolf or human form well…let's just say, he was glad they were on his side.

Moving quickly, and quietly, one to each side of him, they looked at him curiously as he approached home base. Wraithe surprising both of them, and himself, by letting out a growl as they got closer to sniff the small woman cradled in his arms. They eased away to a safe distance, both recognizing the protectiveness of their alpha.

Heading directly toward his cabin, he pulled her slight frame closer to his. He was up the steps quickly to reach his door, shifting her just a bit as he moved to open it, and enter. Taking her toward the back he carefully laid her in his bed, pulling the blanket from the bottom to carefully tuck around her shoulders.

Sensing both of the twins still there, watching in wolf form, Wraithe turned slightly. "Snow, go get Doc." Backing quickly away, and dashing out the door, Wraithe watched down the hallway as, Snow leaped from the porch, and changed back to his human form. Touching gracefully down onto the ground with his long hair flowing behind him.

Glancing at, Hawk sitting there watching, he made the decision to just get it out of the way, and debrief his team. "Hawk, I need you to gather the team, and I want them here yesterday." Wraithe watched, Hawk, while he raced away to follow the orders of his commanding officer. Smiling when, Hawk also leapt from the porch, but unlike his brother he didn't shift back to human, preferring his wolf form. Shaking his head, Wraithe moved to close his cabin door.

∞

The pounding in, Aria's, head was almost unbearable, but she was warm, and snuggled deeper into that comfort, it had been so long since she had felt its embrace. She knew she should wake up, but the blackness wouldn't seem to lift. The heaviness of her eyes was like lead weight. Even the effort to move her body was too difficult. How long had she been asleep? She knew it must be daylight by now, it had to be, and she needed to get moving, had to find a way out. Trying to at least remove some of the stiffness from her body she tried to make her limbs move, but everything felt so heavy. She concentrated on moving her arm, but even it ignored her.

Focusing on her surroundings she did her best to clear the blackness that held her, it was so quiet. Something about that seemed so strange especially in the forest during the day. If you stopped, and listened, you could scare yourself plenty. Wondering what was making the sounds around you, and the not knowing. Thinking the worst could rattle you clear to your bones. Nothing, not even a slight breeze moving through the trees was there. *Oh God, am I dead? Am I just drifting until I find my way to heaven? No, it can't be, I still feel the pain, that's how you know your still alive, right, the pain? What, wait, listening carefully she heard, was it talking, was someone there?* "Please, please she tried to speak, help me." What came from her mouth was so quiet, scratchy, and dry, she knew no one would hear. Taking a deep breath, and willing every last ounce of strength left to her, she opened her mouth, and screamed.

Her eyes finally open, and filling with tears, she watched as men burst through a door to rush toward her. A light came on blinding her, sending electric shocks through her eyes to her brain, not helping her already pounding head. Slamming her lids closed against the shock, someone said. "The lights, turn off the lights."

Gentle hands brushed against her forehead, a deep soothing voice saying. "Hey you're okay, you're okay, just rest, you're safe now." Safe, Aria's mind reeled, she was found, and once again the blackness reached up, and pulled her back down.

Doc checked her pulse, and breathing as, Wraithe kneeled near her head brushing the soft skin with his thumb, doing what he could to ease her. For the first time in, Wraithe's life he had experienced true horror hearing that scream. He was still shaking all through his body trying to assure his beast that she was ok, and to calm. Again not his wolf answering the call, but the beast, it was how he now referred to them, keeping them separate. His wolf whined but the beast. *"Holy shit big guy, you have got to calm."*

Doc nodded his head letting him know all was well. He felt relief flood his body only to look up, and see six men staring down at him. "What?" He asked, staring back at them before, Reaper stepped forward looking down at, Wraithe's arm. Following his friends eyes he looked down, drawing in a sharp breath. Long smooth black hair hung from his arm with long sharp claws once again at the tips of his fingers. "Shit!"

Chapter 2

"How did it go?" He asked, while he turned to face his fellow warrior who was walking into the common room.

"Well my friend, very well." As the warrior took his seat at the long table he couldn't help but smile up at his friend. "The beast emerged, and is more than we could have hoped for. They will have questions."

Wulfgar turned back to the open doors on the balcony looking out into the night. Lost in his thoughts, and grateful the experiment had not failed. Everything now depended on these soldiers, and their abilities. He had to insure their success, and he would do whatever it took to make that happen. This plan had been in the making for a hundred years, failure was not an option.

Turning back to his old friend, he nodded saying "For now we watch only, the time will come all too soon when we will have to explain why, and what we have done." Letting out the breath he hadn't realized he'd been holding, he turned back to the open doors breathing in the forest that lay stretched before him. Wondering to himself how that would play out.

Wulfgar felt a gentle brush against his leg, and without looking down he knew that sitting beside him he would find Star. Solid white in appearance, her eyes lined in black illuminating the jade green color, with a single black tear seeming to drop from her left eye. She was a beautiful animal. To this day he had never seen a more perfect Pit Bull, her bloodline pure, and royal, a gift from, Odin, himself, and she had walked these halls with him for hundreds of years. "Ahh, you always know when I am troubled, always seek me out." Kneeling in front of her to stare into the bottomless depths of her eyes, he raised his hand to run it down her smooth head. As she softly chuffed at him he shook his head, and spoke. "I hope so my friend, I truly do."

∞

Wraithe stared around the room at the faces of his team, no, not just his team, his friends, his brothers. What would they think? Would they believe him or think he had lost his mind, although what more proof could he give them at this time other than what they had witnessed for themselves.

After the young woman drifted back into what, Wraithe hoped, was a peaceful sleep. He had led his men back out into the cabin's living area, from start to finish he had gone into as much detail about what had happened earlier that evening. As much as he could anyway. Still not truly understanding it himself. Looking around he saw questions on some faces, anger on others, and confusion in all.

Reaper slammed his fist down on the table drawing everyone's attention, and said. "More, this is more of what they did to us without telling us!" Fury clearly etched in his face as he stared at, Wraithe. "I don't think so Reaper, I think this is something different, something not even they expected." He stated, as calmly as he could trying to ease his angry friend.

"Why would it show now, it's been five years?"

"I don't know Reaper, I have more questions than you could imagine."

"We should contact control, get someone out here, force them to explain what is happening and why!" Reaper demanded. The anger he felt building at the thought that again he was some damn lab rat under a microscope. It wasn't even that he disliked his wolf, but it had been a long process building a relationship with it, and learning to control it. Now he was faced with something larger, and stronger, it could kill innocents if it got away from him! Once more he was feeling the pressure to learn from the animal because even though the scientists had come up with this experiment, none could answer the questions about how to work with the animal, train it, control it. No, that was left to the men carrying the burden of the animal, and with it, the guilt, if for some reason it hurt someone. Reaper looked back to, Wraithe, his anger clearly etched on his face.

Wraithe saw the pain in his friend's face, understood it. Knowing it was his responsibility, he had to learn how to deal with the beast, and understand why it showed up now so that he could be there for the next man. Catching movement to his right he watched as Snow stood.

"Brothers, I don't think this should be shared with Control at this time." He said, looking down at his twin. "You all know that for, Hawk, and I, the blending of our wolves to our souls was easier, I believe because of our heritage, and beliefs. This new beast I have never heard of, and there could be many reasons why it comes now. I would like to go, and speak with the old ones. If we do not know when this beast will rise, and we are called out on a mission, well my brothers, the damage is unspeakable." He said, turning to again take his seat.

Wraithe had always been grateful for the wisdom that, Snow, always seemed to show in any situation, and this was definitely one of those situations. He looked around the room, and for the most part heard the approvals. The decision was his, and he couldn't find any reason to not allow it. At this time any information, was better than none.

"You leave at first light, safe journey my friends and hurry back." He said, watching the twins stand, and leave to prepare for their trip.

Tired to his bones he dismissed everyone, and prepared to get what rest he could here on the couch. Instead of laying down though, he stood, and began moving toward the room where the small woman rested. *"Mate,"* his beast said, *"little one is mate."* Wraithe felt all the air leaving his lungs on a whoosh as though he had taken a strong blow to his gut. "Mate?" He asked the beast. "What do you mean mate?" Nothing, there was no response, and he knew damn well the beast was ignoring him now. He stood in the doorway staring at her, wanting more than anything to climb up beside her, and pull her close where he could protect her, and give her comfort.

What the hell? He didn't have a clue where these thoughts were coming from, and try as he might to shake off this feeling of protectiveness, it was like it had taken root in him, and was already buried deep. Moving into the room he looked down on her, thankfully, Doc had cleaned her body of the dried blood, and treated her scratches to stop any infection. She was beautiful, with skin that felt as soft as a dove's wings. He hadn't missed her eye color either, earlier, before she was slamming them closed. Green the deepest green he had ever seen, almost shadowed like the color of moss on the rocks just below the surface of the water. Tiny gold flecks sprinkled in like a reflection through the water when touched by the sun.

Wraithe realized he was touching her soft face, lightly rubbing his finger against her soft cheek. A soft moan escaped from between those full lips, and he couldn't stop the groan from his own lips as blood rushed to his crotch. Her sweet scent was like nothing he had ever known, like the forest after a rain. He didn't understand what was happening but it was becoming very clear to him that nothing mattered more to him than her safety, and happiness, nothing.

∞

Aria wasn't sure when the fogginess inside her began to lift, but it seemed like forever. She knew she had to pull herself back up out of the darkness. She was warm, and her bed was soft, cozy, and it had all been a dream, just a dream. Okay so it was more like a nightmare, but it was over, and that relief that you felt when you finally came back to reality was welcome. So was the rush of adrenaline that had her suddenly sitting up in bed looking around to make sure everything was in its place. This wasn't her room, this wasn't her bed. Oh God, what now, she wondered. She moved to push the covers off of her, and realized two things, first she was naked, and second, that the all too familiar ache in every part of her body was still there. She also felt an added weight across her lap that she didn't recognize. Looking down she realized it was a man's arm, and the body attached to it was snuggling closer to her.

Aria threw the unwelcome arm, and blankets away. Yelping as she threw herself from the bed, her legs, and feet not quite understanding what she wanted. She stumbled across the room trying to regain her balance before landing face first against the wall. Turning on shaky limbs she stared back at the bed, and watched as the guy raised up on an elbow, his gaze zeroing in on her. She couldn't help the blush, and the heating of her skin while he looked her up, and down. "Wh…who are you, and where the hell are my clothes?" She blurted out as her body began to vibrate from the exhaustion that she still felt.

"Names, Wraithe, and your clothes, well, they have seen better days." He replied, quietly. "There is a T-shirt there, to your right on top of the dresser." He knew he couldn't make any sudden moves, she was freaked out bad enough. With what she must have gone through, coming across to strong, or quick would send her running faster than a spooked rabbit. She had enough bruises as it was.

Good God, he would remember her body for the rest of his days.

Aria looked down, and grabbed the T-shirt, with shaky arms she pulled it on as quickly as she could. "Where am I?" She asked, but before he could reply she spoke again. "I was lost." But then the shaking through her body intensified, and she felt herself sliding down the wall.

Wraithe watched as the exhaustion took hold of the small woman again, and she seemed to just wilt into a small ball on the floor. Cautiously he eased himself from the bed so he didn't frighten her further. "What is your name?" He asked, softly, as he moved slowly toward her, doing his best to use the most soothing tone of voice that he could find. He was a soldier, for Pete's sake, he wasn't used to speaking softly.

"Aria." She said, watching as he drifted closer to her. He moved so gracefully. She had never seen a man move so smoothly, so fluid. It seemed out of place for him because he was frigging huge. "Please, please don't hurt me." She pleaded, looking up into his eyes. Were those even real, she wondered, or contacts? She had never seen golden eyes before. He just stopped in his tracks, and raising his hands palms out.

"Aria, that's a beautiful name." Wraithe said, kneeling down in front of her. "I won't hurt you Aria, I found you yesterday, and brought you back here to the cabins. I had, Doc, take a look at you, and other than exhaustion, dehydration, and some cuts and bruises, you're going to be just fine. Doc cleaned you up, and put some antibiotic cream on your cuts, and, well, sorry, but he removed your clothes so he could make sure nothing was broken, and there were no other serious injuries."

Slowly easing a little closer to her he asked. "Aria, can I pick you up, and put you back in the bed, you really need more rest? Hey, are you hungry, how about some soup?" Wraithe watched as she slowly weighed her circumstances, he made sure not to move a muscle as she looked around the room. She is so beautiful, long golden curls falling around her shoulders, and down her sides. Those gorgeous green eyes that almost looked as if they were pleading with him for help.

"Okay." She said, so quietly that he wondered if he would have even heard her if it hadn't been for his wolf hearing. "Good, that's good, Aria, I'm just going to reach under you, and lift you up." He said, while he moved over to her, gently sliding his arms underneath her, and lifting easily, she weighed nothing, he thought. Turning slowly he moved her back to the bed, eased her down into its comfort before he carefully leaned over, and pulled the quilt back up around her. "There we go, that's better, right?" He asked, smiling down at her.

He has such a nice smile, warm, and friendly, Aria thought to herself. Cradled for just that brief moment in his arms she couldn't help but notice the hardness of his chest, and arms, how the sudden feeling of safety washed over her, and seemed to ease some of the shaking throughout her body.

"Aria, you rest okay? I'm just going to go down that hall right there to the kitchen, warm some soup up for you, okay? I'll bring you something to drink too, I'm sure you're thirsty." He said, turning to leave the room.

Wraithe moved down the hall toward the kitchen. He knew he needed to talk to her, about what had happened, why she was out in the damned forest, and alone. *"Mate, rest now, no talk, comfort, feed."* His beast chimed in while his wolf chuffed its approval. "Oh now you're talking to me, great." Wraithe bit out as he ground his teeth together. *"Mate too small she must eat, weak, help her."* The beast growled. "What do you think I'm doing?" Wraithe growled back as he began preparing, Aria, something to eat.

As Wraithe moved around the kitchen he knew he needed answers, he just wasn't the type that could wait too long for information. Just as he was about to try and speak again to the beast the beast spoke up. *"I come when mate found, must protect. I always here."* the animal growled. "How?" Wraithe questioned. "Why?" *"Warrior, evil come, only mate can call me forth."* "Well hell!" Wraithe muttered. "I don't want a mate, I'm a soldier, I can be called out at any time, and she will be left alone. You have to understand that, and what about her, she must have a life back wherever she came from."

"No leave mate, must protect, evil coming, I Warrior, I protect."

Wraithe was dumbfounded, "Evil? What do you mean evil is coming?"

"Demons come, mate saw."

Wraithe knew if he were standing in front of a mirror right now looking at his own reflection the shock on his face would have been laughable. With what he had seen in his life he didn't think there was anything left that could shock him. Demons, evil, this day just got better and better.

Pouring the soup over into a bowl after heating it, then placing it on a tray, Wraithe grabbed a spoon and crackers then headed back to, Aria, wondering if she could give him more answers.

She sat propped against some pillows just staring out at the first light of day. It seemed she hadn't noticed his return, she was so deep in thought, and as he watched a single tear escaped from the corner of her eye. Slowly making its way down her cheek to drop unhindered to her arm resting in her lap. Wraithe felt almost choked by the need to offer her comfort, and soothe whatever it was that made her sad.

"Hey, okay, please don't cry." He said in the most soothing voice he thought he had.

She turned her head toward him, raising her eyes to meet his while he moved slowly toward her, setting the tray across her lap. "Thank you? It was all real wasn't it?" She asked softly, not really looking for an answer. Wraithe straightened, and asked. "What happened, can you talk about it?" Aria struggled to form the words she needed, to explain what she had witnessed, how her friends had been attacked, while she watched. Fear overwhelming her as if the nightmare would be real if she spoke the words. She knew though, she knew it was real, but would anyone believe her? Her friends, but not her friends, she couldn't explain that thought. She looked back to the strange beautiful man standing before her, and shook her head no, not now, she just couldn't.

Wraithe watched as Aria's eyes glazed over, and the look of horror that he saw there was startling. Without the slight shake of her head he already knew she couldn't talk of it yet, it was something so frightening to her that she just wouldn't face it right now. Picking up the spoon he dipped it in the soup and brought it to her lips. Looking into his eyes she opened her mouth to accept the offering. As he slipped the spoon from her lips he said. "It's okay, when you're ready, I'll be all ears." He smiled, and dipped the spoon back in the soup.

Chapter 3

"We are grateful for you speaking with us." Snow said, as he, and, Hawk, took their places across the fire from the elders.

White Bear stared across the flames at the two young wolves, and smiled. Easing forward slightly he felt the confusion flowing off the guardians, then asked. "What is it you seek young Guardians, your spirits are tangled with confusion?"

Hawk looked into the eyes of each elder, clear and bright, full of wisdom and so different from their faces that were worn and bronzed from the sun. The crackling fire before them brought, Hawk out of his thoughts, and he spoke. "There has been a change to the wolf spirit of our Alpha. No longer does he walk with one, but with two. The new wolf is different, and moves upright as a man, it speaks as a man, and for now comes forth before he is called. Many of our brothers had a difficult time becoming one with their wolf spirit, they are afraid. We ask for any knowledge you might have to share of such a beast."

White Bear drew back, staring first at, Wahkan, and then to, Ohanzee. Each nodded as they realized the time had come for them to reveal a secret they had long held amongst themselves, since they were young men. War was coming, not that it would be known to the outside world. He had prayed that his spirit would walk with the ancestors before this time came. All their lives, and the lives of many others would now depend on the guardians that sat before them, and the brothers they stood beside. Evil the likes that no man should know, would soon escape its dark place, and spread like a thick fog upon the land.

With a heavy sigh that conveyed the ache in his heart, White Bear stood, and moved to the side of his Tipi where a large bundle lay wrapped in deer skin. Pulling at the leather ties he opened the bundle to reveal the swords placed in his care. "You will take these blades back with you. Each of your brothers must have one, you must begin learning how to use them. Long ago they were placed in my care, and I have dreaded the day that I would have to place them in your hands."

Moving back to his place and seating himself, White Bear began to speak. "Many years ago when, Wahkan, Ohanzee, and I were young men we began dreaming. The dream walkers, we called them, came to us each night, and each night they told us of a prophecy. A time would come when a great evil would find a way to let loose an evil that could take over a human being, and do many wrongs in this world. Turn brother against brother, sister against sister, mother against child. These evils would bring an end to all the world. The dream walkers said that when the time was close great warriors would be brought into being. With them, the first line of the great beast, that would battle these demon spirits. These swords are blessed by the, Great Father, of the dream walkers, and only they can send the demons back to the dark place."

"One by one the beast will reveal itself to you all, but as it does so will a gift from the, Mother Earth, who will send her daughters to you. Each carrying a spirit of the earth to help aid, and protect you. Young Guardians, your time has come, and all of our lives depend on you."

Snow, and, Hawk stared at, White Bear, and knew that what they heard was the truth. Both of them had felt something changing in the forest, but it had been like trying to follow the trail of a ghost. Gone as quickly as it had arrived.

"White Bear, we have felt something changing, and the information you have shared is welcome." Snow said, as he, and, Hawk stood. White Bear, and the other two elders also stood, White Bear moving to stand before them, placing a hand on each of their shoulders. "Trust in your wolves, they know what is coming, believe in them to know the way young Guardians. There is a truck outside that you may take, it will be easier to get the swords back." White Bear stepped back as the twins moved to re-wrap the swords, and then carry them to the truck.

Heading down the mountain in the old truck, Hawk took out his phone to call, Wraithe. Going back this way would delay their return by a day since they couldn't travel cross country. Hawk looked over at, Snow as he maneuvered the truck down the old road in the fading light of day. He didn't have to ask what, Snow was thinking, being twins they had been sensing the others thoughts, and feelings since birth. How could anyone be prepared for what they had just heard, what were they supposed to feel? There was a lot of uncertainty, and just how in the hell were they supposed to prepare for an enemy that they didn't know? Hawk's wolf growled in his head, and took his fighting stance. The wolf knew, and was ready, whatever came they would face it head on. Hawk pressed speed dial, it was time to talk to Wraithe.

∞

Wraithe set his phone back down on the bar in the kitchen. What, Hawk had just told him seemed fantastical. It was time for answers, and the only way he felt he was going to get any was to try and talk with the beast. He moved over to a bar stool, and sat down. Then he reached down deep inside to look for the beast, he didn't have to search far, the big guy was standing there, bold as brass, and by his side was, Wraithe's wolf. For a moment they just stood there taking each other in. Ready to get this started, Wraithe stared at the larger wolf, and said. "Ok, I'm ready to listen."

The great wolf chuffed at, Wraithe, but then lowered itself to a crouched position. *"Many hundred years ago my clan made by, Odin, warriors. Odin make children to watch, protect from times of darkness. We fought with them, send the Great Wolf, Fenrir, back to dark place. Fenrir, great monster wolf, son of Loki, he control evil ones. Door open, and they come, take over bodies, make evil."*

Wraithe didn't know if he could believe any of this. It seemed impossible, demons, they existed? He had never been one to believe in the supernatural, ghosts, and the like, but he never thought a man could be changed into an animal either. A part of his mind wanted to refuse this nonsense, but how could he ignore something that was staring him in the face?

Wraithe stared at the large wolf and asked. "Do you have a name?" The big guy just stared back at, Wraithe, like maybe he didn't understand then spoke. *"I you, no need other name."* Wraithe shook his head, made sense he thought.

"The woman, Aria, you said she is your mate. I need you to explain this." *"Little one OUR mate. She gift, from, Great Mother Earth, little one has magic of earth, must protect, make happy. Must mate soon, bond little one to us. You feel, you want, she made for us, only one."*

"Whoa, there big guy, I don't even know her, she doesn't know me. You can't expect her to just accept this, I mean come on, I can barely wrap my head around all of this." Wraithe said, dropping his head into his palms and rubbing his face.

Anger washed over, Wraithe, so intense it was like little sparks going off in his head, and he knew it was coming from both wolves. Looking back at them they began growling, showing a little fang. "Not you too?" Wraithe said, as he stared at his other wolf. The wolf just stared back as it lowered its head, and then raised it, nodding his approval. The beast straightened, and snorted at, Wraithe. He could swear he saw an eye roll there, yeah this just got better and better, he thought.

Wraithe began to move away having heard enough for now, when the beast stopped him, and spoke again. *"Tell good heart man, no kill innocent."* Wraithe didn't have to ask who the good heart man was, Reaper, yeah he was gruff, and rough around the edges, hell of a fighter, but hurting the innocent, when he was trying to get control over his wolf had been his greatest fear.

He shook his head, and took a deep breath to clear his head, and there it was, that soft female scent. Yep, clean and fresh mixed with just the slightest amounts of other smells of the forest. A light breeze after the rain. Before even realizing what he was doing he began moving his way toward the bedroom. She was awake again, with her legs drawn up to her chest, and her head resting on her knees, she just sat staring out to the evening sky.

Chapter 4

Aria heard him coming her way, she could feel him somehow, knew he stood there at the door watching her. Lifting her head she gave him a slight smile. "Thank you, you know, for helping me. I'm sorry I have been so out of it." She said, quietly, as she stared back at him.

Wraithe thought he could drown in those pools of green, they were even prettier tonight, if that were possible. They were clear now, and not shadowed by the weariness, and fear that he had seen before. He cleared his throat. "You're welcome, I'm glad I found you. Do you know how long you were out there?" He asked, as he moved slowly into the room, and took a seat at the foot of the bed.

"I'm not really sure, three maybe four days. We were camping for the weekend, what day is it?"

Staring back at her, Wraithe smiled. "Tuesday, you said, we, who was with you?"

Aria took a deep breath, and with watery eyes, and a hitch in her voice she spoke. "My friends, there were four of us. This is…was, our favorite time of year to get away up here to the mountains. We've been doing it since our senior year in high school." Reaching up, her small hand wiped at the tear that threatened to fall.

"Aria, where are they, what happened? Can you talk to me about it? I have some friends here, we can go search for them, make sure they're safe."

"Dead, they are all dead." She said, as her shoulders began to shake, and she could hold back the tears no longer. After a few brief moments she took a couple of deep breaths, pulling herself back together.

"I had a headache, when we got here so after we set up camp, I went to lay down in my tent. Marty, Barb, and, Sally were going to hike for a bit, then wake me when they got back. Something outside my tent woke me later, it was almost dark, but I just assumed they had come back, and decided to let me sleep. It didn't feel right, I don't know how to explain it, but all around me it felt…eerie. They weren't talking or laughing as usual, and the sounds coming from outside were more like someone rifling through the camp, throwing things around. I always carry a small gun with me when we come here so I pulled it out, just in case. I lowered the zipper on the tent just a bit at first, to look out, and saw, Marty, and, Barb standing there, they looked almost frozen in place, mesmerized, staring at something over by the SUV. When I looked over I saw Sally, she was." Aria broke a bit in that moment, her eyes glazing over, and true horror shined in her eyes. Tears falling, and her breathing ragged, she struggled to bring herself back to this moment, to escape what she was reliving. "She was stuck to the trunk of a tree, a large stick was sticking out of her chest."

Sobbing now, Aria, could no longer hold back the trembling that took hold of her. The tremors pouring off her body so severe that even Wraithe could feel them from his place at the end of the bed. Sliding up the side of the bed, smoothly he reached out and placed a hand on hers that now rested in her lap, wet with the tears that kept falling. With a slight squeeze to her hands he did his best to offer what comfort, and reassurance that he could.

Lifting her head, Aria stared into those beautiful golden eyes that met hers with such tenderness, and concern. There was just something about him that called to her, pulled her in, and although it was only his hand touching hers it felt like she was wrapped in strong arms, safe and home.

Thinking this way seemed so out of place for her. She had always been more reserved when it came to men, and people she didn't know. Without realizing what she was doing she pulled one of her hands free, and reached up to gently place it against his cheek. What had gotten in to her?

Wraithe couldn't stop the response to her soft hand resting on his face, and pressed his cheek closer, nuzzling the smoothness, and breathing in her soft scent. The calmness that her touch offered was surprising. For this brief moment, all was right in the world, and he wanted nothing more than to pull her into his arms, and hold on to that forever.

Aria pulled her hand away, and placed it back in her lap, blushing lightly at how forward she had been, and lowered her eyes. The trembling had stopped, and as hard as it was she knew she had to finish explaining what had happened. What would he think she wondered, that she was a nut case? What did it matter anyway, what he thought of her, she didn't even know this man, but deep down she knew it did matter, and so did he.

Lifting her eyes back to his she felt a strength, and warmth she had never known, knew that no matter what she said, he would believe her. "I'm not really sure what happened next, it all happened so fast. Marty, and, Barb, both turned to look at me sitting there at the opening of my tent, and believe me when I tell you, I know how this sounds. But their eyes seemed to glow, or maybe it was shimmer, almost like dark mirrors, unbelievable, right? Then out of nowhere, a very large man landed in the middle of camp. He was carrying a sword, a real sword, I swear! Before I knew why, I had slipped out of my tent as this man began lunging, and swinging his sword at, Marty, and, Barb. Each time he lunged, that sword, went through one of them. I screamed for him to stop, but all that did was get my friends attention, and this time when, Marty, and, Barb looked back over at me it wasn't my friends. I mean it was them, but not them! I know it sounds crazy, I mean how could it not be them, but I swear they were no longer there. What was in their place was cold…evil." Breathless, with adrenaline now pumping through her, Aria raised to sit on her knees before she continued.

"The man yelled for me to run, and I did, as fast as I could. I don't know how far I had gotten before I stopped, or how long I had ran, but when I stopped it was pitch black, and I had no idea where I was. I lost my gun somewhere along the way, that's really all there is except for me stumbling through the woods, probably going in circles for all I know. Until I woke up here." Aria nibbled lightly on her lower lip staring at, Wraithe, wondering what he was thinking.

She was right, Wraithe thought, it did sound unbelievable, but with the recent turn of events it also didn't sound as unbelievable as she thought, at least not to him. The beast, chuffed in his head then said what, Wraithe already knew. *"Hunt, must look for door and watch."* Wraithe agreed. He would need to meet with some of his men and go over the information that had been provided so far. Also, who was this large man, and where had he come from?

Thinking and doing it however were two very different things because the longer he was in Aria's presence, the less he wanted to leave it. He thought his dick was going to explode when he caught just that brief glimpse of her thighs moments ago as she moved to her knees. Bringing the very real images of her naked body from earlier tumbling through his head. Mind out of the gutter he told himself. She has been through a lot, the last thing she needs is you pawing her.

Realizing she must be waiting on him to say something he smiled and spoke. "Aria I do believe you. There are some strange things going on around here, and even though I don't have any more details to share with you right now, it doesn't mean I won't. For now I'm going to send a few men to check out your campsite, and the area around it, see what we can find. Can you tell me where it is?" Aria stared back into his lovely eyes and said. "The west side of the lake, the most northern cove."

"Good, that's good. How about some dinner, you must be starving? I have some sweat pants here that might fit you, and I built a fire earlier in the front room. Come sit by it, and I'll fix something for you. That sound okay?" Aria nodded her head, and Wraithe stood to pull out a drawer at the dresser to get the sweats. Handing them to her, Wraithe smiled and turned toward the door. "Just down this hall is the kitchen, shout if you need anything." Wraithe left the room as she stood and picked up the sweats.

Her legs still felt a little sore and weak, but nothing compared to how bad they had been. Moving to the bathroom she found an unopened toothbrush in a drawer and almost jumped with joy. It would feel great to brush her teeth. Moments later she located a brush and did what she could with all her curls but brushing curly hair wasn't the best idea, it would just make the frizz worse. Turning she looked at the shower and decided hot water sounded wonderful.

When the water was hot she climbed in and thought she was in heaven. She washed her face, careful of the bruising and gasped when she looked down at the rest of her body which hadn't fared much better. Next she scrubbed her hair and smiled at the relief of feeling clean for the first time in days. Stepping from the shower she grabbed a towel and caught her first glimpse of all the damage. Eek, horror movie much, she asked herself. Nothing she could do about it now and besides Wraithe had already seen what she looked like.

Aria bent and rolled the legs of the sweats up hoping that would at least keep her from tripping over them. She had folded them down at her waist but she wasn't sure how long they would stay up. Pulling the t-shirt back over her head, and having done all she could to at least make herself somewhat presentable she moved out of the bathroom and down the hall.

The kitchen was pretty large for a cabin, and it opened up into a very large living area. It was surprisingly clean for a bachelor, and the large floor to ceiling stone fire place, and colorful quilts resting across some of the furniture added a warm and inviting feeling to the room.

Wraithe turned and smiled at her. "Hi, go on, make yourself at home over by the fire, stay warm." He said, while he moved to put something in the oven.

"Do you mind if I sit here at the counter?" She asked, her hands went to the back of one of the tall chairs. "I have always felt cozy in a warm kitchen, it's actually my favorite place." Wraithe turned back to her, smiling. "No not at all, like I said make yourself at home." He sat a glass of ice and can of soda down in front of her. "Is this alright, I have some juice if you would rather have it, or tea." Aria moved to pour the soda into the glass. "No this is fine, thanks."

Wraithe began slicing some roast beef while he waited on the rolls to warm. Good grief could this woman be any more beautiful? She was perfection and he had to keep his hands busy or they would be all over her. He had never been so attracted to a woman before, mine, he thought. Shit, where was this coming from? He had always been about the job, the mission. Now this little slip of a woman had him lost in thoughts of wrapping himself around her so that no one and nothing could touch her.

Suddenly, Aria jumped from her chair with a shriek causing, Wraithe to automatically turn into a fighting stance.

"Wait." She cried out, as she looked around, "You said it was Tuesday, I need to get back to Seattle, now! Please, do you have a car? Please, my dog, my dog is in my apartment by now locked in his crate. He was at obedience school, and his trainer was going to take him this afternoon, and drop him off because I work late on Tuesday. I can't believe I forgot, but with everything that happened, I just didn't think." She stated, as she moved around the counter to stare up at him with frantic eyes.

Wraithe let out a deep breath, and although he felt like she had just taken years off his life, he was overwhelmed with relief that she was not in any danger. He could feel the desperation radiating off of her. Slowly raising his hands to cup her face he allowed his thumb to brush over her face. "It's going to be alright, Aria, I will get your dog, little one. I don't think it is a good idea right now for you to be seen. If you should have been back by now, I'm sure someone has reported one of you missing to the authorities. If we get the local police involved it could make matters worse." Wraithe thought he could drown in her eyes.

It's a two hour drive to Seattle, Wraithe thought, but it was still early in the evening so they could get there and back before morning. Wraithe knew she could use some of her own things, and having come up with a good excuse to keep her close at the same time he couldn't help but pat himself on the back. It also seemed to please both of his wolves.

Wraithe lowered one of his arms down around her waist and moved her to walk her back to her seat. "Sit, eat, and then we will head out. You really need to get some food in you to build your strength up. I need to make some arrangements with my team and then we can leave, okay?"

Aria smiled as she took her seat, "Thank you, Wraithe, you really have been so kind, and I don't know how I can ever repay you."

Wraithe smiled back as he moved back into the kitchen. "Hey don't you worry about that, you being safe is all that matters." He said as he pulled the rolls from the oven. Placing two on her plate with the roast beef and potatoes and then setting it in front of her.

"It looks wonderful, and I'm starved, thank you again.'

"My pleasure."

Wraithe watched as she began to eat. He felt an overwhelming need to be feeding her out of his hand. Shrugging the thought away he moved to pick up his phone and call Reaper.

Chapter 5

"Aria, this is a good friend of mine, Reaper." Wraithe said, turning toward Reaper. "He is going to be coming with us, Reaper, this is Aria."

Reaper stared at the young woman, and could understand now why, Wraithe seemed so taken with her. She had kind eyes and a tender smile that immediately put Reaper at ease. He wasn't good with people anymore, not since the change. "Hello Miss." He replied, as he opened the passenger door on the SUV for her.

"Please, Aria, is fine, and it's very nice to meet you too, Reaper."

Reaper nodded as he moved to close the door, then climb in behind her. She had a very pleasing scent, rain, she smelled of rain. His wolf whined then laid down with its head resting against his paws. That was a little strange, normally his wolf was more guarded than that, but if his wolf was calm then so was he. Settling back, Reaper got as comfortable as he could in the back, he was a big guy after all but he would make due. He had been in tighter spots.

Normally it took about an hour to get from base to the road that led into Seattle but it seemed to go by fairly quickly. Reaper must have dozed off because the next thing he knew they were in Seattle and, Aria was giving, Wraithe, directions to her apartment. His wolf was stirring to, the wolf didn't like it when they left the forest, too many lights and people in the city.

Wraithe pulled into the complex where, Aria, lived, and immediately was on alert, something wasn't right. He looked back over his shoulder at, Reaper, and got a nod from him, he felt it to. Following, Aria's, directions he turned down the last row of parking at the back of the complex. The beast growled in, Wraithe's head, but he reminded the big guy that, Aria, didn't know about him yet, and he would scare her. The beast wasn't happy, but he didn't burst out as he had before. *"Demon."* It growled at, Wraithe.

Scenting the air, Wraithe was reminded of decay, something dead was nearby. Aria reached over at that moment and squeezed his arm. "It's Marty's SUV, he is here." She said, pointing toward the large black SUV parked at the end of the drive. Wraithe stopped their SUV and then moved it over to park along the back fence.

"Aria, I want you to stay here, do you understand? No matter what happens do not leave this truck, promise me." He asked, as he looked back at, Reaper, and they began to get out. "Aria, promise me."

Aria stared back at him with frightened eyes, but finally agreed, "Okay, I promise. Wraithe, please be careful. His name is, Zeus, my dog, his name is, Zeus."

Wraithe gave her a tender smile and closed the door, he and, Reaper moving to the back of the SUV. Opening it up they both reached in to pull out a couple of 9mils, nothing special really but they could get the job done.

Both were dressed in black pants, black boots and black t-shirt, blending into the darkness was nothing new to them, as they moved quietly toward the SUV that belonged to Aria's friend. The stench of death only got stronger as they approached. Wraithe passed a large pole, used for lighting the parking area, and noticed glass broken on the pavement just below the light. Someone had intentionally taken out the light.

Using hand signals he motioned for, Reaper, to move to the passenger side of the vehicle while he moved toward the driver side, each raising their weapon as they moved up the sides. There was no one inside but the front driver seat was covered in blood and the smell was even worse up close. This smell wasn't something that was just dead it was decay, rot. Wraithe wrinkled his nose at the strong odor, it burned.

Wraithe motioned for, Reaper, and they began moving off to the left, Aria's place was on the bottom, second door. Listening for any sound coming from inside, they hesitated before trying the door. They didn't have a key, Aria hadn't had one to give them. The sound they heard coming from inside was whining, it was her dog, and it was scared.

Reaper moved to the side of the door with his back against the wall while, Wraithe tried the door handle. It wasn't locked, turning the knob as smoothly as possible he opened the door quietly. Glancing inside he didn't see anyone but that smell, jeez that smell was horrible.

Moving inside they began looking around. The place was a mess and then they heard the growls coming from the back, the distinct sound of a cage being rattled. Silently and quickly they moved toward the sound but neither of them were prepared for what they would see.

Standing over the cage, licking its lips, was the most hideous creature, Wraithe had ever seen. This must be, Marty, or what was left of him anyway. His head slanted at an odd angle and there were pieces of his flesh that looked ripped away, some hanging from his bones.

It must have sensed them because in that moment the creature turned toward them, screeching a terrible sound, it made a rush toward them. Wraithe, and, Reaper, both began firing at the thing, but it just kept coming, only slowed slightly with the hit of bullets tearing the way through what was left of his body.

Wraithe had only a moment before his beast pushed its way through and took over, changing faster than what seemed possible. Lunging forward the great beast grabbed the thing, biting down hard on what was left of his neck and severing the head from the body. It sent both body parts flying in different directions across the room.

Turning to, Reaper, the beast breathed in and said. "Bullets no work on demon, must have sword, take head." Then the beast turned, and opened the cage for the dog. The dog whined shying back in the cage. Making a sort of rolling growl the beast dropped down to squat in front of the cage. Raising its clawed hand into the opening for the dog to sniff. The dog stood and began wagging his tail, now more than ready to leave the cage. When the dog was out the beast softly chuffed and gave control back to, Wraithe.

Smoothly changing back to his human shape as quickly as the beast had appeared, even Wraithe's clothes were there. Okay that was new, and he remembered it happening before when he had brought, Aria, back to the cabins. When they changed back from their wolf shape they were stark naked so this was definitely an improvement. Wraithe stood and stared at, Reaper. Was he in shock, he had never seen a look like that on Reaper.

"It talked, Wraithe, the damn thing talked!"

"Yeah I know, irritating isn't he?"

Wraithe stated as he moved toward the closet in the room to see about getting, Aria, some clothes. Grabbing some shirts, sweaters, and a few pairs of jeans he stepped from the closet. Moving toward her dresser he opened drawers looking for anything else she might need. Wow, this woman really liked her under things. He had always thought you could tell some things about a woman by what she wore under her clothes. For instance with an athletic minded woman you might find more sport bras with only a few sensual items for when she wanted to feel sexy and alluring.

His, Aria, was shy, there wasn't one thong. She also liked the feel of satin against that beautiful skin of hers. No his, Aria, liked boy shorts, styled panties with matching bras and she loved color. Grabbing several matching pairs he stuffed them in the back pack he had found in the closet along with the clothes he had grabbed.

Reaper was staring at the body of what was once, Aria's, friend. "What are we going to do with the body?" He asked as he turned back to, Wraithe.

Wraithe frowned, and decided, on this he should ask his beast. "Well big guy what do you think?" *"Burn it."* He responded back. Great, that's great, Wraithe thought. How would, Aria handle this body being in the back of the SUV until they could get outside of the city to burn it, how was she going to react to her friend being burned?

"I saw a rug in the front room, let's roll it up in that, and get it to the truck, we have to burn it." Wraithe said, as he silently prayed, Aria, could handle this.

They made quick work of rolling the body up, and, Wraithe turned to make sure he wasn't missing anything. Sitting quietly by the bedroom door was the dog, he was a great looking black lab, Zeus, Aria, had said that was his name. "Zeus, hey buddy come on now and we will get you to your master." The dog moved quickly to, Wraithe's side and licked his hand. Guess that means he is ready, Wraithe thought.

Reaper reached down and pulled the rug up over his shoulder. Silently they moved back to the SUV, once there, Reaper, moved to the back with the body. Wraithe opened the back passenger door and watched as the dog jumped up and in. Moving around to the back he helped, Reaper, get the body tucked inside then closed it up tight.

Opening the drivers' door and climbing in, Wraithe placed the backpack in, Aria's lap. "I hope I got everything you need." He said, as he started the SUV and began to turn around so they could get the hell out of here.

"Wraithe, why is my rug in the back?" She asked, as he pulled out of the complex and got them on their way back to base. He looked over at her, then looked straight ahead. "Aria, can I leave it at, I now believe everything you told me? I know that isn't enough, but I need you to trust me when I tell you that, you don't want to know what is wrapped in that rug. I'm sorry, Aria." He slowly looked back over at her and watched as she seemed to accept what he had told her. Tears rolled down her face and dropped from her chin but she said nothing.

A gentle rain began falling on the windshields and he flipped on the wipers. He was proud of her for accepting what he had told her and he admired the strength he found in her.

Zeus softly whined and then moved to rest his head on her shoulder. He knew she was hurting and he did what he could to soothe her. Wraithe reached over and placed his hand on hers resting in her lap. Lightly squeezing he looked back out to the road and pressed down a little harder on the gas. He needed to get her home.

Aria couldn't stand the smell any longer. Reaching over she cracked her window hoping it would pull the odious scent from the vehicle. She knew they were almost back to the cabins but she simply would not take the foulness of what lay in the back a moment more. It was still raining and she took deep breaths of the clean wet air.

The air, for as long as she could remember, it had always brought her comfort. She imagined sometimes that, it came when she called it, when she needed it most. Silly? She supposed it was. Already the nauseous feeling in her stomach was easing, she was grateful. For a moment there she had feared she would need to ask Wraithe to pull over and allow her to empty her stomach.

When she was a little girl her mother had told her that air had a power all its own. She said that sometimes if you listened closely it would sing for you and create a beautiful melody. That was why she was named Aria, her mother had told her. The wind sang the night she was born.

Now, Aria was finding something other than the air that soothed her, Wraithe. She couldn't explain the feeling of peace and comfort that surrounded her when he was near. She also couldn't understand the sense of strong arms wrapping around her when he wasn't close. How could someone she barely knew offer such serenity?

The vehicle pulling off to the side of the road broke into her thoughts. Without anything being said, Reaper, got out and went to the back of the car. Opening it up he removed what was there and headed off into the forest with it draped across his large frame. Aria looked to, Wraithe, but she couldn't make the question form on her lips. She wasn't sure she wanted to know.

Wraithe once more reached to squeeze her hand. "It has to be burned, Aria." Wraithe said as he put the truck into drive and began pulling back onto the road. Nodding her understanding she said nothing and accepted that he was doing what was best.

"Little one brings rain." The beast said as, Wraithe got back on the road, another few miles and they would be back. Reaper would take care of what needed doing and then join them at base camp. In his wolf form he could cover the last few miles very quickly. "What do you mean, she brings the rain?" he asked.

"She is gift, from great Mother Earth and the Mother has blessed her with Air. Scent was foul and she asked air to clean away. When left her home it came to take sorrow." The beast said as its voice drifted softly away.

Wraithe felt like he was lost. There was so much happening right now and taking it all in, well, it seemed he was fighting a losing battle. He knew one thing, he had better just accept it or they were all going to die. This new reality might be more than he wanted, but there didn't seem to be a choice. He was in it now, and had seen too much already to keep denying what was real, whether he liked it or not.

Pulling back into camp he parked the SUV and got out. Moving around the vehicle to help, Aria, he grabbed her backpack and put an arm around her as they moved toward his cabin. He would get her settled and then he would start laying out strategies on how to proceed.

Chapter 6

It was a few hours yet till dawn and the twins should be back anytime, if they weren't already. He would meet with them, lay out some schedules for the rest of the team, and then meet with them all.

Once they were inside the cabin, Wraithe allowed his arm to glide slowly across Aria's back. He felt the slight arch in her lower spine and thought how perfect his hand fit in that space. Reaching for her hand and entwining his fingers with hers he led her toward the bedroom. She needed to get some more rest. Although he couldn't explain how he could feel the weariness coming from her, he knew in that moment that there were just things about her he had to accept. One of them being that she was his, and no matter what, he would not part from her.

Placing the backpack on the bed, Wraithe smiled softly as he looked at her. "You need to climb in this bed and get some more sleep. I won't be far if you need me." He moved to leave the room but Aria's grip tightened on his fingers. Turning back to look at her he was surprised when she moved forward, wrapping her arms around him and resting her head on his chest.

Wraithe moved his arms around her protectively, pulling her in close as he rested his cheek against her head. There were no words spoken. There was only a calming sense of trust. The kind of trust you found when you were in the arms of that one person meant only for you. A kind of strength, born of being united. Wraithe lowered his head and nuzzled closely against her neck taking in her soft scent. He would stand here till the end of time for her, only her, if it was what she needed from him.

It was over all too quickly from his point of view, but she needed rest, and he had work to do. She smiled almost shyly as she moved away and began to turn down the cover on the bed. Ok, he had work to do.

Pulling the door closed behind him he went to his office and began pulling out maps and the other items he would need. He quietly moved it all to the large table in the dining area which fortunately was open to the living area, it would be the best spot for him to meet with his team and cover all the details.

Hearing a sharp knock on the front door he turned as it opened. Reaper, and the twins entered walking up to the table to join him. Noticing the deer skin that, Snow, and Hawk both sat on the floor, he came around the table to look at the contents.

Snow bent and opened the skin, then reached down to take the hilt of one of the swords. Lifting it he handed it to, Wraithe.

Wraithe, didn't know anything about swords but he knew blades, they all did. The one he held was extremely well balanced although a little on the heavy side. The craftsmanship was remarkable and like nothing he had ever seen. The blade perfectly sharpened with some type of symbols engraved down the center on both sides. Looking closer at the hilt he noticed a round disc with a carving that was centered in the crossguard, it looked to be ivory. He didn't recognize the symbol but as he turned the blade he did recognize what was carved there. Two wolf heads facing opposite directions each with their head raised as though howling. *"Not ours."* The beast growled in his head.

Just then Reaper reached down and picked up a sword, the hilt immediately warming in his palm and as they watched the disc at the crossguard turned a deep blood red. *"Sword is Reapers, you try another."* Wraithe's beast said.

"According to my beast that sword is yours, Reaper. I guess each one will react the same as its owner is found." Wraithe said, as he bent to reach for another. Moving a few around he came to one that he just felt was right and upon picking it up the same thing happened as with Reapers. To Wraithe this one felt more perfect than the first he had held.

Wraithe smiled and looked to, Snow, and Hawk. "Okay you two, might as well get it over with. I have a feeling these are going to be our new best friends." He moved around the table to begin reviewing some of the maps as his friends knelt to find their sword.

He needed to expand the perimeter and he needed a team put together to go cover the area where Aria and her friends had been. Recon was always the best place to start, even if you only had a general area. As he finished marking areas on the map he wanted covered his team moved in around the table. Ready to hear the details. When that was completed he would call everyone else in and brief them on everything he knew.

It was going to be a long day.

∞

"I hate that son of a bitch! Master this and master that, yeah I'm going to give him a master alright!" He had, had enough, but right now he didn't have a choice, he was up this damn creek without a paddle.

The team he had now was nothing like the team he was used to working with. This group might be stronger and have more abilities, because of the vile things inside of them, but they didn't follow orders. Don't even get him started on the constant bickering between them! They were like children fighting over anything that another one wanted. He needed some that could think on their feet if plans changed. He couldn't be expected to be with them on every job.

He hadn't signed up for this, but he was in deep. The wolf beast he had been given was extremely powerful, albeit a little bloodthirsty. There were times that reining him in was more than difficult. When he led those hikers to the doorway for the demons it had been hard to keep the beast from raping the women and butchering the man.

He had hardly slept until he had found a place that none of the demons were aware of. It wasn't much, but at least he didn't have to worry about being gutted by one of the damn things while he slept.

It went against everything in him, having to supplicate himself to that fucking master demon, but if he wanted a higher form of demon to get the job done then that was what he had done. The money he was being paid wasn't enough for that shit, but sometimes you just had to suck it up. It worked in the end and he would have the new demons in a week.

Time to start laying out the plans for the next stage. He had to get more people to that doorway.

∞

Wraithe, Reaper and the twins were trying their hand at working with the swords in a small clearing just a short distance from the cabins. In all truth it reminded him more of a couple of kids playing at being knights.

He could feel his beast pulling on him trying to get out. Between working with the swords and fighting the shift his strength was waning.

"Listen," he told his beast, "Things have changed since you were here, its light out now and we can't risk anyone seeing you." The beast growled sharply.

"You wasting time, must learn, I teach."

"My men aren't used to you yet, give it a little time."

"No time left. Not get used to if no see!" The beast howled in his head as it began to push its way out. Wraithe couldn't fight the shift and in just a matter of a few moments, the beast was free.

Wraithe stood there staring out at each of his men as they stopped what they were doing, and stared back at him. He expected looks of shock but what he found were more looks of curiosity than shock.

The twins moved forward, Wraithe hadn't realized how tall the beast was exactly, until they got closer. He actually had to look down farther than he had expected. Most of his men were already tall, six foot plus. By the looks of things, in his beast form, he must be at least seven foot something. He took a moment to look down at himself. Long, smooth black hair covered his body except around his stomach. Although it was still black in color the hair thinned and shortened to reveal at least an eight pack. Heavily muscled arms led to huge hands, with long fingers that tapered to sharp pointed claws. He could do some serious damage with those things. Looking further down he found narrow hips that led to huge muscular thighs. Appearing more like a wolf's body toward the feet as though he stood upright on the pads of his paws with some pretty serious looking claws there as well.

The beast focused on each of the twins, breathing deeply to take in their scents. "Brothers." The beast chuffed while, Snow moved even closer.

"Welcome brother." Snow said, as he looked up at the beast, astonished by its size. The ears were set closer on top of his head, they turned outward and rose to slight points at the top. Its muzzle was long with a smooth fine hair and eyes that almost glowed a hot golden amber. Snow, would guess those fangs were at least three inches.

Reaper, and Hawk, also stepped in closer to get a look at this new beast. They couldn't help but stand in awe of such a creature. It really was a magnificent beast.

"Wraithe why did you change out in the open like this? Damn, are we going to have to fight with this one like we did our wolves to control the change?" Reaper asked, looking up with horrified eyes at the monster before him.

"No Reaper," the beast answered "We come when called. If danger to you or mate, we can take over, but no time now. Must learn sword, I teach so you teach others. Sword kill demon and send back to dark place so not come back. Let soul go of one trapped inside, to be free, go to Great Father."

"So the poor guy last night, you didn't use the sword, you used your fangs to take his head." Reaper said staring up at the beast.

"No could save without sword. Demon come back, soul of man lost. Feel pain of loss, Reaper, but could not save. I regret."

"Then get to teaching because I won't lose another soul damn it!" He shouted as he stepped back and raised his sword.

Chapter 7

Aria woke to the bright morning sun shining through the pains of class in the large window. What a beautiful morning, it was rare to see sun this time of year, especially here in the mountains.

She finally felt rested and she was starving. Climbing from the bed she thought a nice hot shower would do her wonders then some food. Turning, she almost tripped and fell just barely catching herself, Zeus, of course he was at her feet. Laughing she kneeled down to scratch his head.

Raising up into a sitting position he leaned forward to rest his head over her shoulder. It was his way to give her what she thought of as a hug. His soft fur always tickling her neck and cheek. Wrapping her arms around him she squeezed him tight, "Good morning to you to handsome."

She stood and moved to her backpack to find something to wear. Opening it up the first thing she saw was her underwear. Oh good grief she thought, Wraithe had seen her bras and panties, blushing at the thought of him touching them. She wondered if he had liked what he saw.

Aria wasn't sure why she felt so drawn to, Wraithe, but something about him just felt so right. When she had hugged him last night she had felt the strength in his beautiful body. She hadn't ever seen him without clothes but she had a great imagination and it was telling her she would love what she found.

She had fallen asleep earlier dreaming, that she would wake again with him beside her. Maybe he would kiss her, did she want him to kiss her, yes, oh yes that would be amazing. Would he touch her? The thought made her body tingle all over as the excitement of his touches came to life in her mind.

Why did she suddenly feel so hot and her lower half was getting wetter by the minute. She grabbed her soft pink underwear, some jeans and soft pink cashmere sweater, quickly making her way to the shower. Had she thought a hot shower would be nice, maybe a cold one would be better. Nah, she didn't think she could take the cold water but lukewarm might work.

She might be twenty-five but she had never been with a man. Oh she had dates and boyfriends but it just never felt right. Her friends teased her mercilessly, laughing, saying she would be the old woman with dogs living all alone. She'd finally learned just to laugh with them, it was easier than trying to explain how she felt. How could she explain that she just knew it wasn't time?

Thinking of, Wraithe, had quickly melted her body into a bubbling hot mess. This cool shower wasn't helping if she couldn't get him out of her head. She couldn't shake the other feeling either, the one whispering in her mind that he was the one. Another thing was that she had never felt these things. That was partly what she couldn't explain to her friends, other guys just didn't turn her on, ever.

Dressed, she gave herself a last look in the bathroom mirror. Her towel dried curls resting around her shoulders, large green eyes starring back at her, and the soft pink blush to her cheeks, from thinking about, Wraithe, gave her an almost pretty look, she thought. She knew she wasn't ugly but she preferred a natural look which most times made her look younger than she was and sort of plain. She was also short so yeah, no model here.

With a grumbling tummy, she took a deep breath, and opened the bedroom door. When she reached the kitchen and looked around there were no signs of, Wraithe. He *had* said to make herself at home so letting out the breath she had been holding she began gathering what she needed.

Thinking he might be hungry as well when he got back she cracked extra eggs into the bowl after putting some bacon on.

Zeus whined softly as he sat watching her. When she looked over at him he chuffed softly. "Oh Zeus, I'm sorry, where is my head at today?" On, Wraithe, she thought to herself as she moved to take the pan of bacon off the stove. "Outside, is that what you're trying to tell me? Momma forgot you didn't she? Okay, come on, but we need to make it quick alright, I'm starving."

As they moved toward the door Aria glanced around the large open living area realizing she hadn't given it much thought before. Oh my God, had she been in a coma? The door they had been coming and going through was a side door and the exterior porch must wrap around the entire cabin. Smooth planked wood lined the walls around the beautiful stone fire place that was stretched to what had to be a second story ceiling. The light glossy stain on the wood allowing for the natural look of the wood running the rest of the room. With one exception, what she now realized was the front of the cabin which was nothing but glass, even the entry door was wood pained with glass insets.

She loved how warm and inviting the room felt. There was a large leather sofa facing the fire place and large comfortable looking chairs placed closer and to each side, four total. There was also a beautiful table, the smooth surface resting on top of huge antlers.

Zeus whined softly, she turned back toward the door making a mental note to explore more of the cabin later. Leaving the cabin, and jogging down the porch steps with Zeus at her side she noticed more cabins toward the back of this one, not as large she thought but very nice as well.

Turning in the opposite direction she began making her way toward the tree line several yards from the cabin. Watching her fur baby make his way to the trees Aria smiled as a soft breeze swept in to dance around her. She knew she was silly but she couldn't stop herself as she spoke out loud. "Hello, my old friend." Aria laughed at herself as she stopped and took a deep breath, wrapping her arms around her chest, and closing her eyes. Easily sorting the scents that she found, Ponderosa Pine, Fur, and the last of the wild flowers for the season. Was that snow, yes, she thought, as she breathed in deeply, she knew she was picking up just the slightest hint of snow. Aria guessed it would be here tomorrow night and smiled, she had always liked the snow.

Her thoughts drifted back to Wraithe, wondering if she could share her most guarded secret. Her tummy growled again. "Zeus, come," she yelled as she watched him turn back to her and they both headed back to the cabin.

∞

Wraithe was now using his sword to take on both of the twins. He was amazed at the agility of the beast. At one point the twins had backed him against a tree but the damn thing simply jumped up using its sharp claws to secure itself on the tree. Bracing its legs against the trunk of the large pine, then pushing off to jump over the twins, spin in the air and land behind them.

He lowered his sword and nodded to the twins as they lowered theirs. The beast was barely breathing hard but with his knew senses he could feel the strength waning in the twins. Without a thought the beast withdrew and just as quickly Wraithe was back.

"Well one thing that is for sure, the transition back from the beast is easier than coming back from our wolf form."

"The space around you ripples, it is more magic, and the air itself shimmers." Song spoke as he, and Hawk moved to rest on the log where Reaper now sat, watching.

Wraithe thought for a moment and said, "I don't feel any kind of weakness when I come back either. You know, like we feel after being our wolf, the drain. I actually feel stronger and more alert. I'm noticing something else too. When we are in wolf form we communicate telepathically but now I can sense the rest of the team. I know where they are."

"Reaper, you could use some rest so hit the rack. Song, Hawk, I can sense Luca coming in. Once he gets here get him his sword and then send him my way. I need the recon on that camp where Aria and her friends were. I've called the rest of the team back, get them sorted as well. Start with some basic techniques, pair them off and set them to it."

Wraithe turned starting off toward the cabin. He could sense something else to, that he hadn't shared, his mate, she was awake. Immediately he scanned the area for any kind of threat, she was outside of the cabin. The only thing he sensed was his team coming in. He quickly sent them the message to go wide around the cabins. Knowing she was safe was one thing but the thought of her being outside made his insides start jumping around like he was on a caffeine rush. He picked up his pace so that he could be back with her, protect her. "*Calm, his beast said. Wind protect her, little one is safe. Scent air, no smell mate, wind hides her.*" Wraithe took a deep breath as he slowed from the jog he was in. The beast was right, no matter how deeply his breaths were, he could not scent Aria at all.

She was moving back toward the cabin now, the rush to protect her eased in, Wraithe.

It hadn't escaped his notice that he was now referring to her as his mate. He just knew it was true, and yeah, it was really weird. He also wanted her badly, the bulge in his jeans becoming painful. It was becoming more difficult to keep his hands off of her.

Both of his wolves were pressuring him to mate with her. The beast had also told him that he would have to show her both of his other sides. It had to be before he mated with her and bonded her to him. She had to accept the mate bond willingly.

The scent of bacon brought him out of his thoughts, she must be cooking. He felt an overwhelming need to feed her himself, from his own hand. Yeah, weird had officially taken over his life.

He entered the cabin and was greeted by the most breathtaking smile he had ever seen. Walking up to her he pulled her close and lightly kissed her soft lips. "Good morning, did you sleep well?" His response to her had seemed the most natural thing in the world to him. Smiling back at her he knew it had been the same for her. What had it been, two days, and now this, the familiarity that was already between them was more like a couple that had been together for much longer. More than that, it was completely comfortable, and felt right for him to already be greeting her this way.

"Yes, thank you. I feel so much better now. Are you hungry? I haven't seen you eat anything in a few days so I made plenty." Not waiting for a reply she placed several pieces of bacon on a plate with the eggs she had just placed there and then put the plate on the counter with a fork. "Sit please, Wraithe, eat." She said as she turned and prepared another plate for herself and then moved around to sit beside him at the counter.

He smiled at her and took a bite, he was a lot hungrier than he thought. Without a thought he lifted a piece of bacon and put it to her lips. "Aria, please take from me." He said as he watched her open her lush mouth and take a bite from the bacon. "You are so lovely Aria, you take my breath away."

Aria smiled at Wraithe and thought how truly gentle he was with her, although she felt something else to. She couldn't explain it but there was a power in him. Somehow she knew that he would need it, something evil was coming. "Thank you." She said as she raised her hand to his cheek.

"We need to talk about some things, Aria, and there is something that I have to show you. Some of this is so way out there that I don't even know where to start. I have decided that the best way is just to come right out with it, but, Aria, that thought of scaring you, of sending you running from me. Aria, it frightens me more than anything I have ever faced. What I want now is to tell you that no matter what, you are safe above all others to me. I will protect you with my life and if you want to leave me…I will hate it, will do anything to change your mind, but I will take you anywhere you want to go."

Looking into Wraithe's eyes Aria saw only truth. She smiled and softly rubbed her thumb across his cheek. "Wraithe, when I thought you would think I was crazy when I told you what happened to me, you listened patiently, and not once did I see doubt in your eyes. I know you didn't find me at my best but I'm not as fragile as you think. I know what I saw, Wraithe, so how could I possibly run from a man who has trusted me and shown me nothing but kindness?" Leaning forward Aria returned the soft kiss he had given earlier. She sat back prepared to hear what he had to say.

She was amazing and Wraithe felt a sense of pride in his mate, he was an Alpha after all and she would need to be strong.

While they each began to eat, Wraithe started at the beginning telling, Aria, about his team, names, and a little of each of their personalities. Then he told her about the training and what happened next, the creation of the shifter side of them.

To her credit she sat listening quietly, eating her breakfast, with only the lift of one brow marking the credibility of his claim. "I know, I know, now I'm the one who must be crazy, but please let me finish."

He began again with how he had found her, and the appearance of the beast. He let out a loud guffaw at the look on her face. "Yeah, crazy, right?" Wiping all laughter from his face Wraithe spoke again. "Aria, I swear it is the truth, I will never lie to you."

Placing her fork back on her plate, Aria dabbed at her mouth. She replayed everything that had happened in the last week, how unbelievable it had all been, yet...she couldn't deny that it was really happening. How could she then deny that what, Wraithe was telling her was not possible? She had learned a long time ago to trust her instincts and right now they were screaming that this man told her the truth. Hadn't she already felt the evil that was coming? Yes, she had and, like it or not, she was in this now.

Stepping down off the chair, Aria took Wraithe's hand. "Show me." It was all she said as Wraithe slipped off the chair and with his hand in hers he led them to the outside.

"Remember, Aria, no matter what you see, I will not hurt you and neither will what is inside me." He smiled at her, releasing her hand, and then took a few steps away.

Wraithe called his wolf and began the shift. He didn't strip like they normally did, not wanting to shock her with being naked. Relaxing always made this change easier so he did his best to release the tenseness in his muscles. Surprisingly the shift was smoother than usual and he wondered if having the beast had anything to do with it.

Sitting down on his haunches after getting out of his tattered clothing, he starred at Aria trying to seem less intimidating. Of course there was shock on her face but there was something else as well, wonder.

They hadn't realized it but Zeus had followed them out. Silently he had stepped in front of Aria and his hackles raised as he growled. He was letting Wraithe know that he would protect her. Wraithe remained sitting but he was also an Alpha and his wolf growled back asserting his dominance while at the same time sending calmness to the big black lab.

Zeus raised his head slightly and scented the air. Recognizing the dominance of the large black wolf, Zeus lowered his head into a submissive posture and stepped forward. Aria reached to stop him, but the wagging of his tail made her stop. "Please, Wraithe, don't hurt him." She said as, Zeus moved closer to the wolf that had once been a man.

Wraithe chuffed softly trying to let her know that he wouldn't hurt her beloved dog. His wolf on the other hand had to show the dog his dominance, and that he was the leader of this pack. He stood as, Zeus moved closer, allowing the young dog to scent him. Zeus slowly moved around the big wolf then moved back in front of him he laid down, rolling over presently his belly. The wolf chuffed and then moved his great head down to rub along, Zeus's muzzle. Once done he nipped softly at the lab and then jumped around him. Zeus immediately jumped to his feet chasing the wolf.

Aria watched as the wolf and dog played, tussling and rolling on the ground, rubbing against each other. She couldn't help but smile. Never in her wildest imagination could she have thought this up. How was any of this even possible? As wild as it all seemed, it was real and she felt such an overwhelming sense of honor that she was witnessing such a remarkable event.

Wraithe glanced back at, Aria, thinking once again how beautiful her smile was, and how he would do anything to keep it there. He stopped his play with, Zeus, and made his way toward her.

Moving slowly so he didn't frighten her he stopped just in front of her and sat.

Aria moved her hand to just in front of his nose. Her scent, his wolf loved her scent, licking her hand and taking it inside. She knelt in front of him and reached to feel the fur around his neck.

"You are beautiful, Wraithe. Your fur is so soft. Thank you for trusting me with this."

Wraithe moved forward slightly to nuzzle her neck. She giggled as she wrapped her arms around him and squeezed. When she released him he moved away from her once again.

It was time, the beast was pushing to get out and meet his mate as well. He hadn't removed his clothes earlier before turning to his wolf so they were shredded. He had done it because, Aria was shy, and well he really didn't know how to get around that. Now he couldn't change back and talk to her about the beast because he would be naked and wouldn't that just be embarrassing.

Letting out a deep sigh Wraithe let the beast come forward.

Chapter 8

Blackie hung up his phone and slid it back into his pocket. The team of Mercs he had worked with before would be here in two days. He had decided that if he was finally going to get more controllable demons, then he was going to need the right kind of men for them to take over.

He would take them into the woods and get a camp set up near the portal. Tell them it would be their base and where he would be explaining the mission.

It was all coming together and soon he would be able to supply the people to the demon master that he had been paid to provide.

Revenge, a dish best served cold, yeah what the fuck ever! Revenge would be what he had on, Wraithe, and that whole damn team.

Wraithe had been his second, but that last mission together had been fucked up. From start to finish, going after that hostage being held by the Drug Cartel had been a mistake. There had to have been a mole, the cartel was on them almost from the beginning.

The Intel on the hostage hadn't been complete, and what they had found was the hostage, and his teenage son. The cartel had been torturing the kid to get information from the hostage, he'd been tortured as well. They were prepared for the possibility that the hostage might have been hurt so they had brought what they needed to carry him out but nothing for the kid.

Blackie made the decision to leave the kid, he was almost gone anyway. The man they had come for was unconscious, so what would it have hurt? Blackie wanted out of that God forsaken rain forest, and it was looking like they were already going to be late reaching the extraction point. They also had cartel moving in on them, their window of time was closing.

Wraithe wouldn't hear it, wouldn't listen. The whole fucking team took his side. Each of them saying they would take turns carrying the kid. DAMN IT! That would slow them down even more, but Blackie couldn't make them see reason, and it was one order none of them were going to follow.

Sure they had gotten out, kid and all but then, the fuckers, they all had given him up during the debriefing. He was fucked! All over a kid that hadn't made it anyway.

Dis-honorable discharge, he had barely gotten out of being tried and sent to Leavenworth. Wraithe had been given his team, his team!

He had found out later about the experiment, he still had his contacts on the inside. He knew what was going on but he hadn't really believed it, not until he had seen it with his own eyes. To have that kind of power given to them and not him. The anger he felt had become a living thing.

So he had followed them here, watching and planning how he would get his revenge on them. That was how he had stumbled onto that portal. Now he was here, he would have his revenge and sweetest of all he was rich.

Yeah they could shift to wolves, but he had a wolf too and wouldn't those fuckers just shit when they saw his wolf! Now wasn't that just sweet!

∞

Aria couldn't control the trembling that shook her entire being. Standing in front of her was a monster, and if she could have run she would have but her feet wouldn't move. The flight or fright thing, yeah, she had the fright, but the flight just hadn't hit yet. She tried to take deep breaths, God, she tried to remember that it was, Wraithe, but her body wasn't listening and her mind, well it must have shut down.

"Zeus!" She screamed as she watched her lab running up to the monster. When he got just a few feet from it, Zeus just sat, staring up at the thing. Watching horrified as it crouched down, she expected the worst. That thing could rip her dog to pieces with one swipe of those claws. Zeus moved closer and it lifted his hand to rub, Zeus's ears. She was in shock, right, she was seeing things. Was that thing actually rubbing her dog's ears?

"Little one, I no hurt Zeus."

"Oh my God!" She said as she starred at the beast, yep, she was in shock all right. "Did you just talk?"

"Yes little one, I speak."

"Please don't hurt him."

"Zeus met before, when at your den, he know me."

"My, my den?" She asked quietly.

"I let out cage, killed demon."

"Last night, at my apartment you mean? When, Wraithe, and, Reaper went to get him and found my...that thing?" She had almost said her friend, but she knew it wasn't her friend, not anymore.

The beast nodded and as he continued to pet her dog it spoke so quietly she barely heard him. "Yes little one." It said as it stood. It was huge, it had to be over seven feet tall, probably almost eight. To her five foot five she guessed she was little to him.

"Did you just purr?" She asked, as she watched, it stepped closer to her, Zeus at his side.

When he was in front of her he raised his arm to touch her face, and she jerked her head back to avoid the touch. "No hurt little one, just touch. My kind like touch." He said as he began lowering his arm.

She couldn't believe this, but she could actually see the hurt in his eyes. "Wait, it's okay, I just wasn't expecting it." Suddenly remembering what, Wraithe had told her, how this beast had overwhelmed him and taken over. Rushing to find her in the woods, and the care he had used in lifting her to carry her to safety.

Stepping forward she reached for his hand, grasping it gently, she raised it back to her face, careful of the claws. "Thank you." She said as his large hand rested against her face, well the whole side of her head, it really was a huge hand. "For finding me, and bringing me back here."

"Will always come little one."

His little mate was beautiful, her bloodline obvious to him. He stood as still as possible, allowing her to study him. While he absorbed the feeling of her touch from the soft hands that had remained wrapped now at his wrist.

Aria would wonder later what made her do it, but without a second thought she stepped forward to wrap her arms around his lower stomach, and rest her head against his ribs. He had lowered his arm to her back, and as he sheltered her against him she heard his calming purr, which was really a growl she realized. In that moment she felt safer than she had felt since her parents had died. It was a little humbling to accept that this great beast cared for her, and always would. She closed her eyes thinking how wonderfully soft his fur was.

She wasn't sure how long she stood there, holding her beast, and he was hers, she knew that, but moments later she felt a soft kiss on the top of her head. Opening her eyes and looking up, it was Wraithe's handsome face that stared down at her.

"Oh Wraithe," she said, "They are both magnificent." She hugged him to her tightly and was comforted once again as he squeezed her back.

"I was terrified of the beast at first so now I understand why you were afraid to tell me about all of this. Then I remembered what you told me about him, how carefully he had carried me. He was very gentle with me. Are you aware of what is happening when you become one of them?" She just couldn't keep the excitement of what she had seen out of her voice, pulling away slightly so she could look up at him.

Wraithe smiled down at her, happy that she was taking this so well. "Yes, I can see and understand everything, it's still me. As the wolf I have more control but I'm driven more by the instincts that I feel from the wolf. With the beast I'm still aware but he has more control although I'm there in his mind and if I need to come forward, he lets me. I felt it was important that you met them, it's hard to explain because although I'm there they are different. They think differently, act and react differently. And they both care a great deal about you, Aria."

"I like them very much too, Wraithe, and I'm not sure why, really, but I feel comfortable with them."

Wraithe pulled away from her slightly but kept her tucked snuggly against his side while he turned to walk back to the cabin.

Wraithe could sense Luca coming toward them and stopped at the porch to wait. "One of my guys, Luca, is coming in, do you mind waiting?" He asked as he stared down into her beautiful face. Again he just couldn't help himself as he leaned down to lightly place a kiss on her lips. God, they were soft he thought, and he wanted her so badly. What he wouldn't give at that moment to be in bed with her, exploring every inch of her, tasting her, loving her.

Hearing someone clear their throat, Wraithe looked up to see Luca, standing there staring at them with the biggest shit eating grin he had ever seen plastered all over the guys face. The guy could seriously be confused with the Cheshire Cat, from frigging Alice in Wonderland.

"Luca." Wraithe said, as he stepped back to Aria's side. "How did the recon go on that camp? Did you find anything out?"

Luca, straightened and got serious. "Wraithe, there is some damn, ah sorry, darn weird crap going on out there man." Luca said as Aria let out a giggle.

Wraithe smiled, and looked at Aria, then back to Luca. "Luca, this is Aria, Aria, this is Luca. He is a member of my team and the one I sent to check out the area where you and your friends were camped.

Aria reached out her hand toward, Luca, and spoke as they shook hands. "It's okay, Luca, I have heard worse language, and I've used it to. It's very nice to meet you."

"Nice to meet you, Aria."

"Wraithe, we need to talk."

"Go ahead Luca, she knows everything. You already know that was her camp you went to check on, and she witnessed what happened there, so speak freely."

Luca straightened and looked at Wraithe. "Well first off there is nothing there that would make you think anyone had been camping on that spot recently. No tent, no vehicle, not even a set of footprints, there weren't any tire tracks either. The whole place was wiped clean. There was a fire there but it has been out for several days. I could tell there had been some kind of scuffle but not much else. Funny part is I can sense something, well my wolf can and he doesn't like it, not at all. I picked up the scent of blood on a tree and followed it for a while but then it just disappeared. There was no trace left, nothing. Wraithe, there is something bad out there, I can feel it, my wolf can feel it and I'll tell you brother, it's freaking creepy."

Wraithe had felt it when, Aria stiffened beside him at the mention of the blood. He knew she was remembering her friend being stuck to that tree. Where had everything gone and why wasn't there a trace of it?

"Thanks, Luca. Get with the twins and make sure the guard on the perimeter is doubled from now on. I don't want anyone running alone, and pull it in closer to base during the night. Did you get your sword?" Wraithe asked as he stared at Luca and moved to pull Aria closer.

"Yeah, I got the thing. I'm gonna go back, talk to the twins to get this set up, and then I'm going to work with them on learning how to use the dam........darn thing." With that, Luca turned and headed back to the clearing.

Wraithe pulled, Aria, close and turned to head up the steps and into the cabin. "I could use a hot shower, do you mind?" He asked, while he closed the door behind them. "I won't be long."

"No, not at all, I'm sure you could use some rest to. I haven't seen you get any sleep since I woke and found you in bed with me." Aria, choked on her own words and blushed. "Hmm, excuse me, I'm just going to get something to drink." She said as she brushed quickly by him and headed for the kitchen.

Wraithe laughed to himself, yeah, that blush covered her whole body, he was sure, and he remembered clearly how it made her skin glow.

Chapter 9

Wraithe stood under the shower head, his palms against the tiles, head bent. He was doing his best to control the urge that was overtaking him, his need for his mate. His wolf was growling, pushing to take her and the beast, well the beast was flashing memories at him. Her scent, the way she looked without her clothes, the softness of her skin. He had turned the water to cold because even his cock was pushing him to make her his.

He didn't want to rush her, the reality was they had only known each other a few days, regardless of how quickly they have become comfortable together. He could smell her need, knew right at this very moment that she was as wet for him as he was hard for her.

Wraithe was so lost in his want of her that he hadn't noticed she had come into the bathroom, he didn't move, too afraid of startling her. What did she want? God, he was losing it and the last thing he wanted was to come at her like the wild beast that he was.

Aria stepped into the shower, she was so afraid he would reject her but she had lost the will to hold back, and she didn't have a clue where this boldness had come from. She might be shy, she might be a virgin, but this man, he was hers, and she wanted him, and she wanted him now.

"Aria, please, I'm losing what restraint I have left." Wraithe said, then pressed his forehead against the cool tile. "Did you know that I can smell you, that I can feel your need so deeply it's like a fire burning out of control inside me?"

She blushed at, Wraithe's words, but she had never heard anything sweeter. Moving closer she reached up between his shoulder blades, and then rubbed outward admiring the broad shoulders and the ripple of muscle under his skin. He was so incredibly well made, perfect in her eyes. Aria pressed herself against his back and rested her cheek against him while her arms wrapped around him.

Wraithe took a deep breath and held it, her hands were silk against him. Her body curved and shaped perfectly, and he could feel it all as she pressed herself to him. Her full firm breasts pressed against his back were driving him crazy. He let out the breath he had been holding, forcing his muscles to relax and uncoil. Pushing away from the tile he turned slowly hoping he didn't break the hold she had around his waist. "Aria." He said, not even recognizing his own voice, as he looked down into those dark green eyes that he knew could mesmerize him. Lowering his head he kissed her lightly on the forehead then began moving down to tenderly place them everywhere he could, her eyes, nose, cheek, before reaching those lush full lips.

No longer able to hold back he took her lips and released a passion that he didn't even know he had. Pushing his tongue into her mouth to twist and turn, to taste. She was glorious and he pulled her in tighter as he forced his kiss deeper. She returned his kiss with the same frantic need, raising her arms to his shoulders, rubbing them, pulling him in closer.

Wraithe broke the kiss long enough to lift her off the ground, sliding her higher up his body. She reached into his hair and took hold of a fistful to force his lips back to hers while he left the shower, her legs wrapped around his waist, rubbing herself against his hardness.

Their tongues continued dueling as he lowered her to the bed and followed her down. He moved slightly to her side to keep his weight off of her but also so his hand could roam down her side, feel every inch of her supple body. When he reached her lower thigh he grasped behind her knee to pull her leg over his waist. He just couldn't get close enough.

Running his hand back up her body he let his fingers just barely graze the softness of her skin. She giggled into his mouth as the goose bumps raised on her skin while her body quivered. Breaking the kiss, Wraithe smiled at her before he buried his face in her neck, nuzzling her and breathing in that clean freshness of the forest after a rain. Finding that tender spot where her neck met her shoulder he kissed and licked the spot. His bite would go here, not this time, not yet because she had to willingly mate him, but this was the spot.

Wraithe pushed back against his wolf, it was pushing to come forward to mark his mate. The beast was pressing him to bond. *No! He told them, willingly remember, she has to accept this willingly. Soon.* They backed off but they weren't happy about it, they stayed just below the surface, waiting. Ready to take their mate.

His hand had reached her breast, closing over it, squeezing, then moving away to play with her nipple. Wraithe kissed down her body, no longer able to ignore the nipples that waited for his kiss. While his tongue played with one nipple his hand had moved to the other. He pinched it lightly, tugged on it, and all the while he was enjoying the soft moans that escaped his mate's lips.

Each moan from her felt like it went straight to his cock, making it harder, thicker. He wasn't sure how much longer he could hold on. He wanted her too badly. The air was thick with the scent of her need. Her body shifting and pushing to get closer, her hips raising in the air, seeking the one thing it needed most at that moment.

Aria couldn't take this sensual attack from, Wraithe any longer, she needed him in her, driving into her. Giving her that fullness that her body was begging for. "Please, Wraithe, please." She moaned softly as she reached for his manhood. Finding what she was looking for she wrapped her fingers around him, well she tried. He was thicker than she had imagined and inwardly she was pleased while wondering to if it would fit. Velvet, the skin was softness covering steel and she was going to die right here if she didn't have him in her soon.

Releasing him she braced her arms on his shoulders and pushed, rolling him to his back while she came up and seated herself across his abs. She rubbed her wetness against him and he moaned as he felt the heat. Aria had no idea where this boldness was coming from but she was glad for it. It was like another side of her was waking. Yes, she was shy, but it was a mistake for anyone to take that as weakness, she was far from weak.

While, Wraithe moved his hands to her hips she moved back until her wetness slid across that velvety steel. She stared into his liquid gold eyes and dared him to stop her from taking what she needed. Rubbing her clit against him she was the one moaning. Reaching down she grabbed his cock and put it against her opening so she could lower herself onto him.

He was really thick, and it took her a moment to work the tip inside, but once it was there she moved up and down against it. She knew she was tight, after all she'd never had a man here before. Slowly she was able to take more of him within her and it was a torture to them both, they were panting. She could see the strain in, Wraithe's face and knew he was holding back. She had to make it fast, it would hurt less. As quickly as she could she forced herself down on him, she couldn't stop the small scream that escaped her as she was finally seated fully on him.

Wraithe was in shock, he had felt that inner resistance as she had forced herself down on him. And while it was the most amazingly wonderful feeling to be buried in her tight heat he worried that she might be hurt. Before he could ask if she was okay she began moving. Lifting herself slowly and then lowering back down. She was the most beautiful thing he had ever seen as she rode him. He brought his knees up so that he could brace her back but also so that he could push back into her as she lowered back down against him.

Raising her arms and running them up through her hair, she stretched her upper body as her pace quickened. Her movement so erotic he didn't know how much longer he would last. Wraithe tightened his grip on her hips as her ride became wilder, harder. Her moans and the calling of his name was driving him mad. He pushed harder and deeper, giving her what she wanted more of.

Aria was about to explode, the sensations of Wraithe being buried in her, hitting that spot over and over again that brought her closer to release. Looking down at him she thought he was glorious with the light sheen of sweat covering his chest. Her gaze moving up she caught and held his gaze. She had never seen a look like that on a man, desire, hunger. The muscles in his neck and chest hardening as she rode him.

She moved forward to lay against his body and claimed his mouth. The kiss was frantic and so were their bodies together, her pushing back hard against him as he drove deeper into her.

It was only moments before she felt the clenching of her muscles and the explosion in her body. Wraithe wrapped his arms tightly around her and thrust harder and deeper into while her body screamed in what she thought could only be rapture. She felt his release and reveled in the feeling that he had also found his pleasure in her body. Without thought her body clenched tighter to hold onto him, not wanting to let go.

With both of them breathing heavily Wraithe couldn't stop himself from pulling her even closer against his body. He had never experienced such pleasure. His arm began to rub up and down her small body and he realized how perfectly she fit against him.

As long as he lived he would never forget this night.

Aria raised slightly to look at him and asked, "Am I too heavy?"

"No beautiful, you're just right."

Aria laid her head back down against his chest, just under his chin and he felt her yawn. "Sleep, Aria, I'm here." Wraithe said, brushing her hair up away from her back and pulled it over his other shoulder. He turned his head toward her hair and closed his eyes. As he drifted to sleep he thought he had never felt anything so right.

∞

Reaper had only managed an hour or two of sleep. He had never really needed much and with everything going on it made getting sleep even more difficult.

He had always liked working with leather, making belts, wallets, knife covers. So as usual when he needed to relax or think, he turned to his leather work. After some thought he had worked some nylon straps and leather together for a way to carry those swords. They needed a way not only to carry them as humans but they had to be able to carry them as wolves.

Every time he thought of the soul of that young man that had been lost, his stomach turned. If he believed all of what Wraithe's beast was telling them, then they need to be prepared and it was much more likely they would come across those things as wolves than as men. Especially here in the forest, the portal for those damn demons was here.

Using his own sword for measurements he had created a type of harness that slipped over his head and across one shoulder. There was a leather strap to catch the sword at the crossguard to keep the sword against his back and shoulder, the blade would slip into a leather sheath, and then a smaller strap stretched down to snap securely around his upper thigh. This piece kept it secure at his back but he hoped as a wolf it would be easily carried along the side of his body. They were much larger than normal wolves so he hoped he had the measurements right. Now he just needed to shift and try it.

Reaper grabbed up the sword and strap and headed to the clearing. It was late evening but with his wolf's hearing he knew the rest of the team were still there practicing with the sword.

When he reached the clearing he stopped to watch. All of them were adjusting well to the swords. It was surprising if he were to be honest, none of them had ever worked with this type of weapon before so how could he not be surprised at how well all of them seemed to be taking to it. He was also pleased, with what they would be facing, they didn't want to go up against these things with untried weapons, it would put them at a huge disadvantage.

Noticing, Hawk, and Snow, standing over by a log observing the team as they worked, he began making his way toward them. Catching movement at the corner of his eye he looked over to see, Wraithe also entering the clearing.

Before Wraithe even reached them, Reaper could smell the sex all over him. What was weird was that, Wraithes', and Arias', individual scents had blended, Reaper's wolf whined in his head, *mates.* It was a very nice smell, the perfect mix of his wild musk and her fresh rain. It was calming, even comforting. Reaper's wolf was bowing and moving his head to the side.

By the time, Wraithe reached, Reaper, and the twins, everyone was staring at him. As Wraithe turned in a slow circle looking at each of them, they dropped to one knee and each held out his sword, bowed his head and leaned it slightly to the right, giving access to their throats.

Wraithe was stunned, what the hell was going on? His beast spoke up, *"It is honor to you, promise to protect you and mate. When bond she will be Alpha female."* Once again, Wraithe looked around but he didn't know what to say so he said the only thing he could, "Thank you."

As if it had been nothing they all stood and went back to what they were doing.

Snow placed his hand on, Wraithe's shoulder speaking softly. "We could smell the blending of your scents brother, and I can't explain the rest except to say our wolves compelled us to kneel and honor our Alpha."

Wraithe cleared his throat a little, then asked, "You, ah, you mean you smell that we had sex?" Well of course they could, what had been thinking. Running his hand through his hair, which felt longer than usual, he thought to himself, damn, I knew I should have showered. He just hadn't been able to do it, he wanted her scent on him.

"Yeah, things are just getting weird around here." Reaper said, as he handed Wraithe the harness he had made for the sword. "What do you think? I'm going to put it on and see how it works when I shift. I figured we would need a way to carry the swords."

Wraithe looked at what Reaper had handed him and thought it was perfect. Reaper was creative as hell and this harness would come in really handy. "It looks great, Reaper, let's see if it works."

Reaper had already undressed while Wraithe was looking at the harness. Taking it back he slipped it over his head and right arm, pulled it down along the side of his body and secured the bottom strap around his upper thigh. Then he called his wolf and began the shift.

He was pleased that the harness hadn't interfered at all with his shift. He could feel the weight along his body but his wolf didn't seem to mind. He stretched out his body and then began to move around. There were no restrictions in his stride that he could feel as he ran around the clearing, jumping large ferns and small bushes. As he had hoped the hilt of the sword lay over his shoulder blade and didn't restrict the movement of his neck and the tip of the blade didn't slip from the sheath that rode at his thigh near his hip. He ran back to, Wraithe, and looked up at him.

Squatting down, Wraithe once again looked at the harness and as he pulled and tugged to test the strength he was pleased with the work. "It's a great idea Reaper, and it looks like it will hold up really well. As soon as you can you need to make up one for everyone and a few extras."

Reaper released his wolf and shifted back, as he stood the twins moved up to him to pat him on the back, complimenting him on the harness. He removed the harness and handed it to them for a closer look while he redressed.

Once more he caught movement out of the corner of his eye and looked over as his wolf scented the air. There was no scent which was very strange but sitting there in the tree line was a large white dog. It just sat there staring at them. He wondered if maybe it was lost so he knelt down and patted his thigh as he called to it to come. The dog tilted its head to the side, like it was considering the request, but made no move to approach them.

Wraithe walked over to, Reaper, and stared out at the dog as well. It looked like a pit bull. They called to it several times, but still it just sat there, staring at them. As an Alpha, Wraithe thought he would try moving closer while he sent waves of comfort to the dog. It was a female, and yes a pit bull, but no matter how much reassurance he sent to her that she wouldn't be hurt, still she wouldn't come to him. He managed to get within a few feet of her and then squatted down and called to her again. Nothing, just that stare. He was struck with the feeling that he was looking into the eyes of a very old soul.

Her eyes were green, not like, Arias', deep green, but light green. It was like looking into pools of jade hidden under a silver mist. Wraithe had faced down some stares in his life, but this, this was like his soul was being studied. Maybe it was because of the connection through his wolf. There was no sense of feeling threatened coming from her or even curiosity, it was more like he was being judged. It was a little unnerving to say the least.

The beast had taken notice as well and Wraithe could swear he felt recognition coming off the beast, but he wasn't talking. Instead, the beast went to one knee, and bowed his head, placing a large fist over his heart.

Without warning she began to run toward, Wraithe, but as she reached him she leapt over him and quickly ran toward the other side of the clearing to dart into the forest and then she was just gone.

Wraithe looked down as he started to rise and noticed something else that he could add to the list of puzzles, she left no prints. There was nothing to mark her presence, not even a scent.

"Alright big guy, cough it up. What just happened?" He asked his beast.

"No threat, brother." The beast responded, and then broke the connection.

Wraithe knew he would get nothing more from the beast, and somehow it didn't matter. He had a feeling he would be seeing that dog again.

Chapter 10

When Wraithe got back to the cabin he found, Aria in the kitchen, making salad. She smiled that beautiful smile as he came in, the one that lit up his entire world and he couldn't help smiling back.

"I have some potatoes baking, and I'm hoping you have a grill, I took out some steaks earlier, please tell me you have a grill."

Walking up behind her and placing a hand on the counter to each side of her he nuzzled her neck then whispered in her ear, "Yes love, I have a grill and steak sounds great."

Arias' entire body came to life and her toes curled in her shoes. Laying the knife down that she had been cutting tomatoes with she turned slowly. "Hi," it was all she could say as she looked up into his eyes. They were hungry again and she knew it wasn't for the food.

Wraithe lowered his head so his lips could taste her sweet mouth. He wrapped his arms around her and pulled her close. She melted into him, molding her body to his. God, he thought, I just can't get enough of her. When he was away from her it took everything he had not to rush back to her side. Sure it had only been a few days but already she was everything to him.

Aria felt like jelly when she was in his arms. There wasn't a part of her body that didn't want to be touching his. His simple touch could fire her blood so deeply that already the all too familiar wetness was back as her body cried for him. Reaching down she found the hem of his t-shirt and pulled it upward and he broke the kiss only long enough to pull it over his head to throw it to the floor. She loved the feel of his body, the muscles rippling underneath her touch.

Wraithe reached down to her ass and lifted her up his body. Her legs wrapping around his hips pulling him closer against her body. He could smell her need and feel the wetness that already soaked her jeans from that hot sweet place. Every part of him craved her lush body. What he wanted now was that sweet scent all over him, he needed to taste her, to draw that sweet honey into his mouth.

Breaking the kiss, Wraithe starred into her eyes and asked, "Are you sore? Aria, you were a virgin and I completely neglected asking you earlier if I had hurt you."

Silencing him with her finger to his lips, she smiled. "Shhh, Wraithe, I'm fine. I was the one that took you, and although I'm a little shocked by my actions, nothing has ever felt so right to me. I wanted you then and I want you now. I can't explain what I'm feeling, how I know this is exactly where I'm supposed to be."

Wraithe listened carefully and decided it was time to tell her what the beast had told him. Besides the damn thing was howling in his head to tell her and his wolf was snarling that it wanted its mate.

"Aria, I'm so new to all of this, the animal side of me. It was one thing to be experimented on and changed to a shifter but I had no way of knowing how it would affect me in other ways. Both of my beasts are telling me that you are my mate, that there will be no other woman for me. I honestly don't know what all that means but I do know that you mean more to me than my own life. I can't and won't ever let you go."

"My parents died in a car accident when I was fourteen, Wraithe, and since I had no other family I was placed in one foster home after another. Some were okay and some were really bad. I was in one of those bad ones when I started high school, that's how I met Marty, Barb, and Sally. They made my life bearable. By my senior year the beatings had become so bad that I ran away. Sally and her family took me in and for the first time since my parent's death I was happy, but Wraithe I always felt like something was missing. I know all of this is so strange and I can't explain some of the things that I'm feeling either, but here with you, I feel like I'm finally home, that I'm safe. Together we will figure out the mate thing. Wraithe, I feel you are mine too."

Wraithe pulled her close, hugging her tightly. "There is a search party up north, they are looking for all of you. A few of my guys spotted them this morning. They shouldn't come down to this area, it's protected. There are two packs of natural wolves that have been transplanted into the area. As far as anyone knows, we are here to study them and protect them. I want you to be careful though, when you're outside, just in case they do come down this way."

"My friends families, oh God I wish I knew how to help them. I know they are all worried out of their minds but after what happened, the thought of them being told that horrible truth. They can never know, Wraithe, never. I couldn't live with myself if they ever found out."

Wraithe pulled away from her slightly and tucked one of her beautiful long curls behind her ear. "Don't worry little one, no one will know. Now, let me get that grill going so I can get you fed, and then we can pick up where we left off." He said, as he wiggled his eye brows up and down.

Aria giggled as she released her hold around his hips and slid slowly down his body. She turned and said, "Do you have more firewood? We need to build up the fire, it will snow by early evening tomorrow."

"Yeah, it's stacked right outside that side door on the porch, he said, pointing to the door next to the kitchen. I will bring more in after I start the grill. Hey, how do you know it's going to snow?" He asked, making his way toward the side door just off the kitchen.

"Okay, it's silly but when I was a little girl my mother used to tell me that if you listened closely the wind would tell you things. She would make a game out it. When she was gone, and I needed to feel close to her, I would play the game and "Call the wind" as she used to say. Earlier today I took, Zeus, out and the wind came rushing to me. It felt like it was saying hello. Look, I know it sounds stupid, and like a little girl telling stories but it felt like it whispered "snow" to me and I could swear I smelt it in the air."

"Beautiful, if you say it's going to snow then I believe you, and I don't think you are silly." Wraithe said, turning the handle on the door and stepping outside to start the grill.

As he was getting the grill ready his beast broke into his thoughts. *"Need show little one not game, wind will come when she calls, protect her, tell her things."* "I know," Wraithe said, lowering the lid on the grill. "I'll get her fed and then bring her outside. You will have to come forward, this is one thing I can't help her with."

Dinner went well, Wraithe thought, that is if he could convince Aria that sitting in his lap to eat all the time was a good thing. He couldn't help it, there was just a compulsion to feed her from his own hand, to make sure that she ate well. To be honest even though he carried a wolf in him, he really didn't know much about natural wolves. This had to be something from them, a way of caring for their mates.

It was cooler outside now that the sun had gone down so he insisted she put on a quilted flannel jacket he had hanging by the side door. Wraithe flipped on the outside lights, he rarely used them because of his wolf's night vision. With, Zeus, at their heels they stepped out onto the porch. Zeus darted down the steps and headed for the tree line.

"Aria, earlier, are you sure you are comfortable with the beast?" Wraithe asked as he placed his arm around her waist and pulled her close.

"Yes, I am, and I really wish you wouldn't call him the beast. Doesn't that offend him or something, I don't know, maybe hurt his feelings?"

Wraithe laughed. "Well I guess I can see how you would think so, but he doesn't seem to mind and with two of them, I had to call him something to separate the two. Aria, make no mistake, he is a warrior, he will kill and kill brutally if necessary, and so can my wolf for that matter. You understand that don't you?"

Aria starred out into the night, thinking over what, Wraithe had said. "Yes, I think I do. It's just that it has been such a lovely day, for a moment I forgot what is going on out there." She looked back to, Wraithe.

The corners of his mouth lifted slightly as he pulled her tighter against him. "Okay, here is the thing, what you told me earlier, about the wind, well the beast says it's more than a game. He wants to come out. There are some things he needs to show you. Are you okay with that?"

"What do you mean, it's not a game?"

"I honestly can't explain this to you, Aria, I can't show you."

Aria pulled away from him and headed down the steps of the porch. Looking toward the tree line she noticed she couldn't see, Zeus, he was black after all and just blended in with the shadows, he was out of range for the outdoor lights. "Zeus, come." She called and watched as a dark shadow moved away from a tree and began moving toward her. After reaching her, Zeus took his place at her side and sat.

She wasn't afraid of the beast but so much was happening so fast. It was like being in a nightmare from which there was no escape. Granted not all of it was a nightmare, her being with, Wraithe, was the most wonderful thing she had ever known. If someone had told her a month ago that werewolves and demons really existed, she would have laughed in their face and offered to take them to a hospital for help. Now, well she was a little shocked at how easily she was accepting it. As much as she wished otherwise, it wasn't a nightmare, and she trusted, Wraithe, to know what was best.

"Alright, Wraithe, I'm ready."

Chapter 11

Wraithe stepped down off the porch and moved in front of Aria. He had watched her as she had drifted off, deep in her thoughts. He could feel that she wasn't afraid, it was more overwhelmed than anything. Warning his beast to take it easy on her he let him come forward.

When the shimmering stopped the beast stood where there had once been Wraithe. Stepping forward, Aria, moved to him and raised her hand to his chest to place it over his heart. She could feel the heavy thump as it beat against her palm.

"Hello, Warrior." She said, craning her neck to look up into his face, and smiled.

Bending, the beast nuzzled his head into the hair at her neck. It was just like Zeus when he gave her his hug, and she giggled, yes, okay, she was a giggler. Reaching with her other hand she raised it to the other side of his head and smoothed the silky hair. He smelled just like Wraithe, that wild musk, it reminded her of the forest.

"Little one." He spoke as he pulled back from her and stared into her eyes. "We begin, little one. So much change for one so young. I regret more must be told, time short. You must be ready."

"Long ago great Odin create wolf warriors. He also call to great mother of earth, ask her help. She create daughters of earth. Daughters are mate of wolf warriors, only they bring out beast from man. Daughters given gift by great mother, can speak to magic of land. One gift to each. Air, your gift, little one. I teach."

"Wait, what do you mean, air is my gift? Do you mean I'm some kind of witch? I have read books with witches in the stories, I don't know anything about calling the corners."

Aria, stared at the beast like he had grown another head, thinking how really impossible this sounded. What she had done with her mother was just a childhood game, something to tease the imagination of a child. She had always been a rambunctious kid. Getting in trouble for not thinking, just following where her curiosity would lead. After her mother was gone she had rationalized that calling the wind was a way to calm her down, and teach her so she would think before she acted. It also had made her memories of her mother clearer, and it helped her to feel closer to her.

"Not witch, Fae and Druid, little one. You come from very old bloodline, Keepers. Protect land for Great Mother." The beast pulled, Aria, close again, carefully hugging her. He would have spared her this but there was no time. She was being asked to understand so much in only a few days. But he also knew that she was stronger than she thought. She would be an alpha female and she would be the life, the nurturer of her pack. He took a deep breath and softly growled for his little mate, the purring as she called it, seemed to calm her.

Wraithe felt, Aria relax against the beast and he knew she was thinking over what the beast had told her. It was as if while thinking things through she braced herself for what was to come and he knew in that moment that he loved her. His wolf chuffed at him as if it was saying "it's about time" and he smiled to himself. He watched as she pulled away from the beast, ready to face what she must.

Drawing her shoulders up and back, Aria, shook herself and cleared her thoughts. "Okay." she said, "Let's do this. What do you want me to do?" She asked, there would be time later to think all of this through.

Moving to stand beside her, the beast looked down at her and said. "How do you call wind?"

"I don't really call it, not any more, like when I was a kid. When I come outside I just feel it, it moves around me. I'm not sure how to explain what happens, it brushes my face like a tender kiss, or when it's feeling playful it ruffles my hair. Look there, at the plants." She said as she pointed to plants in front of the porch. "They aren't moving, so there is not a breeze but I can still feel it touching me. It will bring me the smell of flowers when I'm sad or having a bad day."

"That is good, Little One." The beast spoke softly. "Now ask it bring you small breeze, but use hand as speak, show what you want. Wind learn too."

Aria, thought for a moment and then raised her arm, with her hand sideways she moved it softly like a conductor of an orchestra might move his hand, just a smooth slow wave. As she began she softly spoke the word, "Breeze."

She watched as the air around her began to move. First the limbs of the bushes by the porch and then she could hear the rustle of the leaves in the trees as they brushed against each other softly. The limbs of the branches seeming to moan as their leaves reached up to take flight. The tall ferns brushing against the ground, and grasses, as well as the bark of the trees that they nestled against adding their soft whisper of "ssshhh".

Aria smiled saying, "Thank you, my old friend." She raised her other arm, clearly speaking, "Lift." As her palm faced upward, elbow bent she drew her palm up higher in the air. The sound around her grew and she laughed as the lower heavier branches creaked and groaned while they lifted from below.

"This is so amazing Warrior," she said, turning her brilliant smile on him "but how can this be happening?"

"Ahh, little one the gift from Great Mother strong in you."

Aria turned back and slowly lowered her arms, as she did the breeze faded away and the stillness of earlier returned to them. She stepped in front of the great beast and looked up to smile at him. "Thank you." Speaking the words so quietly while she stepped even closer to hug him.

The warrior raised his arms and carefully wrapped his little mate in his embrace. So much was to come in this war, so for now he would not take for granted these quiet moments with her. Ever would she be precious to him. Moment by moment he could feel the strength growing in her and he was filled with so much pride.

Raising his powerful head he took a deep breath and howled at the sky, singing to the Great Mother his thanks for this blessing.

"Must practice much, little one," he said, and then he was gone and Wraithe stood in his place, smiling down at his sweet mate.

"It's getting late, you can practice more tomorrow." He said, turning with her snuggled against his side they made their way back inside, Zeus trailing behind.

Aria, felt the heat of a blush on her skin as, Wraithe led her to the bedroom and began lifting the hem of her sweater. She might want him more than anything but this need for him was still new to her.

Wraithe watched the rose tint blossom on her skin as he removed her clothes. She was the loveliest thing he had ever seen. In his career he had traveled to many places, seen some amazing sights but nothing, nothing could compare to the beauty of the woman who stood in front of him. Inside and out she was beyond compare.

"Aria will you mate me? You must willingly accept the bond. I know it all seems so fast between us but when I told you before that there will never be another for me, I meant every word. One lifetime with you will never be enough and I will gladly stand beside you for the rest of my life."

Aria watched as the moisture gathered in the golden eyes while Wraithe spoke. He hadn't said the words, I love you, but what were those three small words compared to what he had said? She had never heard a more beautiful declaration of love than what had just been spoken to her.

Throwing her arms around his neck and pulling him down close, her lips pressed to his and she did her best to throw every ounce of love she felt for him into that kiss. "Yes, Wraithe, yes I will be your mate." She panted the words, after pulling away from the desperate kiss.

Reaching for his t-shirt she grabbed on and quickly pulled it from his body as she felt his fingers grazing her back to unclasp her bra. Removing each other's clothing was done slowly and tenderly while they touched or kissed softly at places that sent shivers down the other.

In just moments, Aria found herself once again laying on the bed with Wraithe above her, showering her body with kisses, each one placed so gently that her body barely had time to respond to one area before she was feeling his lips in another.

Adjusting his body to slip between her legs at just the right angle, he began a slow torturous lick upwards toward her clit. Once there he wiggled his tongue just above it causing her hips to lift upward. Her hands clasping at the sheets before finally moving to grab his hair. Wraithe had wrapped his arm around her hips to keep her just where he wanted her. He settled in, determined to coax as much of that sweetest rain from her body as he could get. Releasing his hold on her slightly so that she could work her hips enough against his tongue to find the pleasure that was building quickly in her body.

Her moans and pleas grew louder as she begged for release and when she raised her hips again he pushed two of his fingers deep into her. When the scream escaped her lips and the explosion of her release overtook her, Wraithe quickly raised above her placing his cock at her opening and plunging hard into her depths. Her body buckled and she arched forward grabbing him to her.

Wraithe couldn't stop the need to drive harder and deeper into his mate. He feared he was hurting her but there was no controlling this, his wolves would bond with their mate tonight.

Pulling from her quickly and turning her over he raised her hips to once again take his thick length. Again he drove into her over and over again. She pushed back against him, meeting him stroke for stroke, crying for more. As he felt her tighten around him, so close to her release, his fangs dropped from his gums and he reached forward to move her curls to one side. Lowering his body against her back he licked and stroked the spot on her neck where his mark would go.

Faster, pushing harder and faster against her he stopped to rotate his hips while her body clenched and tightened in release.

Grinding against her Wraithe felt his own release as he bit down against her neck and shoulder. Once more her body clenched his cock while she found pleasure again, screaming his name.

Wraithe, pulled from her body and moved them both so he could spoon against her back while he licked and kissed the spot on her neck. He listened to her panting and moaning as her body slowly relaxed against his. Pulling her closer against his body, mine, he thought, and both his beasts howled in his head.

He could feel the waves of happiness and a sense of completeness coming from his mate. Smiling into her hair he took a deep breath. Their scents had mingled again but were somehow stronger this time. They blended so easily together, becoming one, just as their souls had just done.

"I love you, Wraithe, I love you." Aria spoke softly, turning in his arms to face him, placing a tender kiss against his lips.

"Aria, my love, my mate."

He raised on his elbow and moved her hair away from her shoulder. What he found shocked him and he moved quickly over her to get a better look. "Dear God, Aria, are you all right, are you in pain? Oh my love, never would I have hurt you like this if I had known." And while he looked back and forth between her shoulder, and her eyes the wound began to heal. The bruising was fading, punctures closing, leaving only the scar of where his top canines had entered in the front and his lower canines in the back.

Aria sat up to face, Wraithe, and calm him. She placed her hand on his cheek and looking into his eyes she spoke. "Wraithe, I'm not hurt. When you first bit down it gave more pleasure than pain, but I won't deny that it did sting just a minute while you licked it. Now it doesn't bother me at all. It's okay, Wraithe, I'm fine."

Wraithe, grabbed her and pulled her to him, hugging her tightly. "You're sure?" he asked. "I'll call Doc, let him have a look."

"Wraithe, it's late, I'm tired and I promise it doesn't hurt at all." She said, pulling away from him to lay back down, yawning.

He reached down and pulled the sheet and quilt around them as he snuggled in behind her, pulling her tightly against him. Satisfied that she was safe he closed his eyes, relaxing against her. Listening as her breathing deepened he knew she was fast asleep and he thought about how much had changed in just a few days.

Mated, he was mated and would have to take precautions to make sure she was safe when he was away. Tomorrow was a full moon, it was the one time that none of them could stop the change, they would be in their wolf forms for several hours. Aria, had told him it was also going to snow, not that it mattered to their wolves. He would stay close but he needed to tell her not to leave the cabin.

Chapter 12

After showering and dressing Aria made her way to the kitchen to see about fixing something to eat. For some reason she was starving this morning and since Wraithe had taken, Zeus, out already she could whip up breakfast now, which really was a good thing because her tummy was seriously growling, too bad it was too early for a steak.

Moving around gathering what she needed her thoughts strayed to last night. Feeling herself blush at how he had loved her all through the night. She had never dreamed that making love with someone could bring about such a feeling of completeness.

She had always been so jealous of her friends, listening to their sexual exploits and the thrilling nights filled with passion. Never had she let herself dream that it could be as wonderful as what she had experienced last night. But somehow she knew that if it had been anyone, but Wraithe, the experience would have left her wanting.

The way he had touched her, the tenderness, the urgent passion, the way he had her soar higher and higher until she thought her world was going to explode.

"Aria, love, you have to stop thinking this way or I will be back to ravish that sweet body of yours, again." She jumped, turning quickly, thinking Wraithe had entered the cabin. *"What the hell, now I'm hearing things."* She thought, grabbing the counter to steady herself.

She heard, Wraithe laugh and then speak again. *"Ah, love, no, you aren't hearing things, it's me. We are mated now and I guess this is a wolf thing, I can hear your thoughts loud and clear in my head. Before we mated I could sense you, where you were, how you were feeling. I can talk with my team the same way, fortunately they never think such wicked things about me."*

"Wraithe, I'm not sure I like you being in my head all the time. A woman needs her privacy, especially when it comes to her own thoughts."

"Don't worry, little one, I can't hear your thoughts all the time, you were just thinking so hard about me that it was like you were calling to me. You will learn to control it. How are you this morning, my love?"

"Happy, but starving. I was fixing something to eat, now how do I get you out of my head?"

Wraithe, laughed again and broke the connection.

It wasn't just her alone against the world any longer and without any doubt she believed that no matter what lay ahead, Wraithe, would always be by her side.

The toaster popped, jarring her from her thoughts and she looked down surprised to find that not only was her food ready, but it looked like she had fixed enough for an army. What the hell was with her today?

Well, let's see she thought, as she sat down to eat, in the last several days she had lost her closest friends to demons and if that wasn't scary enough, so was the realization that demons existed. She had also found out that shape-shifters and werewolves existed and she was now mated to one, of course that was also the best part because she had found the man of her dreams. Then on top of all of that she had found out that she was also a mystical type of creature herself, some kind of fae, a keeper, and could control air.

She dropped her fork and rested her forehead in her hand. It didn't seem right that she wasn't freaking out over this whole thing. Aria thought back to the first time she had made love with, Wraithe, that feeling that had overwhelmed her. She had felt something waking within herself, but what it might be, she still had no idea. Perhaps it was the fae side of her or maybe there was more of her that had yet to reveal itself. A person could really go a little nutty thinking about all of this but deep down she felt stronger than she ever had in her life. Come to think of it, she knew exactly who to ask.

Aria cleared her mind and thought of the beast, she pictured the way he looked, the heavy beat of his heart against her palm and the softness of his fur. *"Warrior, can you hear me?"* She asked, centering her thoughts and reaching out to him.

"I hear, little one."

"Warrior, I have some questions, and thought maybe you might have the answers. I feel like something is awaking in me, another side of me that I didn't know was there. Do you know what it is, why it's happening now?"

Aria heard the other wolf in Wraithe whine and then chuff at her. Smiling she offered him her greetings as well and pictured herself running her fingers through his soft fur.

"Little one, you are female alpha and keeper. Must be strong for your pack, soon other keepers will come."

"I don't understand, what do you mean alpha, and what pack?"

"Wraithe, alpha, his warriors, wolf, he leads. I alpha, my warriors come when more keepers come. You our mate, you lead females, nurture pack."

"I lead the females? I don't know anything about being a leader, wait lead them in what? And what do you mean I nurture the pack?"

"You will know to lead, that is waking in you, little one. You bring calm, peace. Heart is big in you, little one, others will need. So much you have learned, harder for new keepers, you help."

"Wow, that's kind of a lot to take in, Warrior. I hope I don't let you down. I guess I still have a lot to learn so I better get to it. Thank you." She said, breaking the connection and thinking over everything the Warrior had told her. Time to go get some practice in

with the wind, she had a feeling she needed to get as strong with it as possible.

It was dusk when, Wraithe found her and Zeus. The day had really gotten away from her, but she was proud of herself and what she had learned today. She had done her best to perfect her talent with air, not only by speaking the commands and using hand gestures but also by just using her hands. She was sure there was more she would need to learn but she was satisfied with what she had accomplished today.

There was something that was making her feel twitchy, and as the evening began to settle around them the anxiety was building in her. It was so bad now she thought she was going to come out of her skin.

Wraithe did his best to calm her down since he thought maybe she was getting nervous about him running with his team tonight. She would be alone except for, Zeus, and he assured her that he would not be far from her.

Maybe she was getting a flu or something. She was starting to ache all over but she wasn't running a fever or showing any other signs. As a matter of fact she was already hungry again and she and Wraithe had just had dinner an hour ago. She knew, Wraithe could feel her anxiety and she could feel his worry for her.

Doc had been called and checked her out but couldn't find anything wrong with her. Maybe this was a sign of some sort, like a warning of some kind. She had started to pace now, she just couldn't sit still.

Wraithe stepped in front of her and as he spoke he palmed her cheek. "That's it, I'm not leaving you. I cannot stop the change because of the full moon but I don't have to run. Zeus, and I will both keep you company. Besides both of my wolves are refusing to leave you, well the beast is anyway. I'm not sure what is up with my wolf, he is acting funny, not like he is nervous or on guard, but excited. He is jumping around like he wants to play." Wraithe, smiled and laughed a bit.

Aria smiled up at Wraithe. "Thank you, for staying. I don't feel like anything bad is going to happen but I have never felt anything like this before."

"Aria, it's time for me to change, but I'm here, you can talk to me through our link, remember?"

"Don't worry handsome, I'll be fine." She stepped back as Wraithe began removing his clothes. Damn, but his body was fine! He was all golden except for his hair, it was black as a ravens' wing, and muscles, yeah, he had muscles on top of muscles.

Moving to the sofa she sat down as her legs began to cramp, even her hands and arms were starting to hurt. Not wanting to worry, Wraithe, any more than he was, she held back the moan from the pain she was beginning to feel throughout her body.

Feeling a soft nudge against her thigh she opened her eyes and looked at Wraithe in his beautiful wolf form. She couldn't hold back the moan that escaped her lips, the pain was becoming more than she thought she could take.

"Aria, what's wrong, my love?"

Wraithe couldn't believe what he was seeing, Aria was changing before his eyes. Her body shifting and stretching. In just moments standing in front of him was the most beautiful wolf he had ever seen. She was snow white with touches of silver and a darker grey around her ears and around her throat. Her green eyes made all the more alluring by the color of her wolf's coat. Holy shit, he thought.

His wolf immediately took over, rubbing against her. Then licking her muzzle and face. Zeus moved over to see her as well but was quickly put in his place by a sharp growl from, Wraithe.

Aria chuffed at, Wraithe, and then moved toward, Zeus. She was a little clumsy at it but it was different learning to walk on four legs instead of two, Wraithe remembered it all too well. She also still had pieces of her clothing still wrapped around her body.

"Wraithe, what has happened?" she asked softly in his head.

"I don't have a clue, Aria. It has to have been the mating, the bite. I'm so sorry my love, I had no idea this could happen. How do you feel, are you alright?"

She wiggled out of her remaining clothing and then sat, looking down at her paws. She turned her head from side to side, taking in her new look.

"Well, this is different." She said, and then laughed. "Do I look okay?"

"Oh my love, you are beautiful. I've never seen a wolf as beautiful as you are."

"Well, it's starting to snow outside so at least I will be warm." She said, as she glanced over at the large front windows and then back to him.

"Aria, you are amazing, did you know that? With everything that has happened, with all that you have had to deal with this last week, God, I love you!"

"And I love you too. Now, take me for a run, I feel wonderful." Speaking softly as she stood and then stretched out to lean forward against her paws. Her rump sticking up in the air, Wraithe groaned to himself, he needed some cold air.

Wraithe headed for the side door with, Aria, behind him, Zeus bringing up the rear. Using his teeth to grip the lever handle he pulled it down then pulled the door open.

As, Wraithe took off into the forest, Aria, and, Zeus followed. In her mind, Aria pictured the lovely white wolf in her head and it seemed to be urging her to move faster and come along side of Wraithe, her place at his side. Loping quietly through the forest, Aria was amazed at the sights and smells of everything around her. She felt the wind move up around her and ruffle her fur, her old friend had joined them as well.

The snow was falling heavily now but she wasn't the least bit cold, her paws seemed to fly across the snow as Wraithe picked up speed and then they were running. Gliding through the darkness as if they had wings. Her eyesight sharpened and perfect for seeing what lay in front of her. Her muscles lean and strong as they lifted her up and over a fallen log. It was the most glorious experience of her life. There could not be a greater feeling of freedom than what she felt right now.

Wraithe nudged her with his shoulder, turning her in a different direction. Soon they reached a small clearing and he slowed and came to a stop. Zeus came up beside her, nipped at her neck and took off, and the next thing she knew she was chasing him, and, Wraithe was chasing her.

They jumped and rolled and head butted each other as they played in the snow. She couldn't remember the last time she had, had so much fun.

Aria, wasn't sure how long they played before her ears began to twitch. Her wolf stopping and listening to the sounds of the forest. It only took her a moment before her eyes caught on an owl perched nearby, its long talons gripping the lower branch of a large cedar. It sat watching, unmoving and quiet. As she watched the owl it appeared to take notice, and starred back at her. Its eyes unblinking. She wasn't quite sure what it was, but there was something different about that owl.

She was broken from the spell as Wraithe moved against her side. His much larger frame rubbing against her. He laid his much larger head across the back of her neck, and softly chuffed at her. Aria thought that, if she were in human form, this would be where goose bumps would raise on her skin. Her wolf gave only a soft rolling growl, Aria had come to call purrs.

Her mate began licking her ears and then moved to her face only to rub his muzzle along hers. Her wolf began to respond in the same way. Rubbing her face along her mates, then moving to rub her own body along the length of his.

She guessed all good things really did have to come to an end because before long, Wraithe was rounding them up and heading them back the way they had come.

Aria could hear sounds coming from where they were headed, she felt her wolf tense, raise her muzzle to the air, and then come to a stop. Other wolves, Aria sensed from her wolf. "Wraithe?" she spoke softly across their link.

"Don't worry, love, it's my team, in their wolf form."

"Okay, I understand but I don't think my wolf does."

Wraithe had never considered that. There had never been any issues with him and his team when they changed, but they had all changed together, knew each other. None of them had ever had to welcome a new wolf to the pack.

As the twins, and, Reaper, moved quietly from the cover of the forest, Wraithe warned them across his link, they needed to come in slow. His wolf seemed to recognize what was happening and growled softly at them. This was definitely uncharted territory for them, but he sensed their wolves would know how to handle this.

Snow moved forward first, slowly, and lowered his head as he approached, Aria. The closer he got to her the closer he also got to the ground until he was pushing himself along, crawling on his belly.

Aria watched as the beautiful dark grey wolf approached. Her wolf seemed to ease a bit after scenting the air. The grey wolf stopped and lowered his head to rest against his paws. Aria's wolf moved toward him and began scenting him, moving around him slowly. She could smell him and other wolves on him, it was as though her wolf was marking the scent as friend, pack, is what came to her mind.

Soon the other large grey wolf and the large blonde wolf moved forward. It went faster this time as she moved quickly around each, having recognized their scents. Her wolf seemed to mark the three as beta and with that, the rest of Wraithe's team moved into the open. Her wolf marking each scent as they moved around her. Wraithe gave her a name of each of the wolves across their link as they had passed.

Wraithe chuffed and the wolves formed around them as he once again headed into the forest. Aria, and, Zeus, following. The other wolves taking up positions beside them and to their flanks. Aria picked up her pace, and she once again took her place beside her mate, followed by their pack.

They reached the cabins in no time at all and Aria had to admit to herself that she regretted being back. It meant a return to reality, and although from what they could tell, things were quiet in the forest, her time with Wraithe was precious, she knew that soon all of that would be changing.

Her wolf took the lead and rubbed against her mate, they would be parted from each other for a time in their wolf forms. Aria sensed the sadness in them, Wraithe licked her face and then turned to head up the steps of the porch and into the cabin.

"Wraithe, how do I change back?" She asked, watching as he moved in front of the fireplace and sat down.

Wraithe watched, Aria come and sit in front of him, starring into his eyes. "Clear your mind, my love, and think of your human self. Push forward in your mind and let your wolf recede." He watched her closely and as the shift began he also let go of his wolf and once more took his human form.

He knew she would be exhausted after her first shift, it took a toll on the body and the mind, especially in the beginning. Standing he walked over and pulled some large pillows from the floor by the fireplace and placed them all around her, glad that he had built the fire up before he had shifted. He laid down beside her and pulled her close. She was already asleep but snuggled closer against him as he tightened his hold on her. Content that she was safe and warm, Zeus resting at her feet, he too allowed sleep to take him.

Chapter 13

The next several days passed quickly and Wraithe was beginning to feel more comfortable not only with his beast but with the new game plans that had been initiated.

New perimeters had been set, both for day and night. Escape routes planned for areas in the forest, back to the camp, and worst case scenario, evac routes from the camp. A large cave had been found higher up on the mountain and was currently being stocked with supplies and weapons. Every weapon was cleaned, checked and rechecked. Strategic weapon stashes were placed throughout the camp and forest. The decision not to booby trap areas in the forest had been made, an innocent civilian or the wildlife being declared an unacceptable casualty.

His team was also, more. More, what a word to describe what they were. Once they had been considered elite, what word could describe them if they had surpassed that? Yeah, more just seemed to be the word.

His pack had begun to master the sword, thanks to the beast, not to mention it had also been explained to them why that sword was important. Unless that sword severed the head from the body of the possessed that person's soul would be forever trapped in the underworld, and the demon who had possessed the person would be free to take another soul. Not one member of his pack were willing to accept that outcome.

The twins had also pointed out to him that more often than not, he was referring to them as the pack, he wasn't even aware it was happening. He would admit that he was starting to feel closer to his wolf sides. They were becoming one instead of three.

After, Aria's, shift, Wraithe had to explain what had happened and why. If what the beast had told him was true, and he believed it was, then all of the guys would soon be finding their mates as well, and their beast would also come out. Some of the guys didn't take that news to well. Wraithe pointed out that it might not happen for all of them, and even though it could be tomorrow, it could also not happen for years. For now that had worked to settle them.

They all worked longer, practiced harder and if not sleeping they were performing whatever duty was theirs on the rotation. Somehow one of their duties was to keep an eye on Aria. Not that Wraithe cared, it made him less edgy knowing that at least one or two of his pack were with her when he couldn't be. It had just seemed strange because he hadn't assigned them that duty or asked them to do it.

Aria, didn't seem to mind either, she felt she needed to get to know them. So if she wasn't practicing with the wind, or shifting to her wolf, she had someone to talk to, she had said. It had actually worked out better than Wraithe had imagined, Aria tended to wander when in wolf form, caught up in all the sights and smells. This way if she strayed she wasn't alone or unprotected.

He had almost come unglued when she had wondered off a few days ago. He had sensed when she changed, they had discussed it, and he had reminded her to stay close.

Wraithe had been in the middle of training with his sword, concentrating on mastering it, he hadn't kept his connection open with her. The next thing he knew his wolf was howling in his head.

Within moments he had shifted to his wolf and was running to his mate. His wolf having sensed his mate in danger, it was a pack of natural wolves and she had apparently stumbled onto them.

Being an alpha female the unmated alpha of the natural wolves had decided to claim her. When she wouldn't submit, and he caught the scent of Wraithe's wolf, marking her as mated, the natural wolf had no choice. He would have to force her submission, she was on his territory, once forced into submitting he could claim her. If she didn't submit, he would kill her.

When, Wraithe arrived, Aria, and the natural wolf were snarling at each other, the alpha preparing to make his move and tackle her.

Aria wasn't sure what this wolf's problem was but he was really pissing her off. Okay, she was willing to admit that this was her fault, her wolf had tried to warn her not to follow the scent of the wolf she had picked up, but she pushed her wolf into it. She was curious, and just like when she was a kid, that curiosity had gotten her in trouble.

Well come on she thought, how was I supposed to know the stupid wolf would want to mount me? She sure as hell wasn't having any of that and neither was her wolf. All she could do now was let her wolf take the lead and deal with the situation. Mentally she slapped her forehead and admonished herself, yeah, now you listen to your wolf, idiot!

Aria had known, Wraithe, was on his way, had known when he got there, but she wasn't prepared for the sight that greeted her now. The huge black wolf stepped slowly from the cover of trees. His head lowered, growling deeply, fangs barred. Every step seemed calculated and precise, the hair along his neck and back raised in warning. He angled himself at her side, but not close enough to touch, and faced the other wolf, giving a kind of part growl, bark, and snarl once he came to a stop. Aria felt like she had been transported onto the scene of an Animal Planet documentary.

Her wolf eased back to her mate's flank, her breathing calmed as she too watched for what would happen next.

Wraithe was furious and so was his wolf, there was no calming things down now. Shit, he knew they were on the natural alpha's territory but he'd be damned if he ever let another man take Aria, let alone a wolf. He also knew what this would mean when they fought and they would fight, there was no getting around that. The natural alpha was now defending his territory and the right to lead his pack. It wasn't like Wraithe could sit him down and work things out.

He was going to walk away from this with something he didn't want and shouldn't have. Alpha, of a natural wolf pack.

"Wraithe, hey, Wraithe, you okay man?" Reaper was asking as he shook, Wraithe's shoulder.

"Yeah, sorry, just deep in my head I guess. What's up?"

"The cave is all set. We got the last of the supplies moved up there."

"Good, glad to hear it. How was it with the natural pack up there?"

"Fine, with winter coming on I think they are happy to have a den. This pack hasn't been in the area long enough for them to have found a place to hold up for the colder weather. They haven't had a chance yet to put on weight for it either." Reaper brushed his hair back out of his face, securing it with a strip of leather.

"Wraithe, these idiots that are transplanting these wolves don't seem to be thinking about things like that before dropping them off here. I set a few haunches of venison out up there for them to find, see if I can't get some weight on them. The elk are starting to move so it won't be long before the pack is hunting the herd."

Good heart man, which was what Wraithe's beast had called Reaper in the beginning. Yeah, Reaper was a one hell of a guy. Ruthless fighter, deadly, hence the name Reaper but the guy had a huge heart.

"Thanks, Reaper, let me know if you think anything else needs to be done." Wraithe spoke, as he turned and headed to the cabin, a little alone time with his mate now on his mind.

∞

All of the mercs were now here and currently setting up camp. Blackie was pleased, so far, by the guys and the equipment that they had picked up. Mack, a big hulk of a guy, was the most experienced so Blackie had appointed him the leader for this team. Yes, everything was coming together nicely, he thought.

They needed a day or two, get used to each other and their abilities. Finish setting up the camp and getting some plans in order.

Once the demons took over these bodies, they would know what the person they possessed knew.

The portal would be opened in a few days, all these men would have passengers. Blackie shivered, he wasn't a squeamish man but the thought of one of those things crawling around inside him really gave him the creeps. Whatever, it would get him to his goal and that was to end Wraithe.

His best chances now to build the army that he needed, and was being paid very well for, was to first begin taking over some of the smaller towns. Putting some of these guys in key roles within the towns, and then placing more demons into the bodies of the top officials of these communities.

That damn master demon had told him that at some point it would be taking a body. Hell that was all he needed, that freak in a body. The upside was that as the smaller towns were being taken over, the master demon would be busy in them, opening portals. Good, the farther away he was the happier Blackie would be.

He had already run this area, where the camp was set up, he knew Wraithe's team was already patrolling nearby. His wolf had scented them. He had about a ten mile border in between them but he was still edgy about that. A shift in the wind, while Wraithe's team was on patrol, could easily provide the location of this camp. Now with this damn snow falling the chances were definitely not in Blackie's favor.

Yeah, he needed to step things up, he thought as he turned to look for Mack.

∞

Luca and Thumper were just leaving the cabin as Wraithe arrived. "Hey guys," he said as he climbed the porch steps, "all done?"

"You bet, all done and it's covered up back in the rec area." Thumper replied, he smiled at Wraithe with a knowing look.

"Thanks guys, any problems keeping her out of the way?"

"Nah," Luca answered. "Doc, came by while we were bringing it in and he kept her busy working on her magic. We will see you in the morning, Aria wants to have a breakfast for everyone. She asked us to tell the rest of the team."

Wraithe smiled, his little mate was something else, she might be younger than the rest of the pack but she was doing her best to mother them. "Okay, sounds good. Thanks again."

"Hey, Thumper, did she get it out of you today? Did you tell her where you got your name?"

Thumper smiled his big old smile and just laughed. "Nah, she didn't get it out of me, but she sure tried." Still laughing he turned, slapped Luca on the shoulder and they headed out.

He looked around as he entered the cabin but didn't see Aria. Pulling his jacket off he hung it next to the door just as Aria came out of the walk in pantry carrying an arm load of something from the freezer, the meat wrapped in white butcher paper.

Moving quickly he made it to her just as she was trying to drop her cargo on the counter. "Aria, what is all this?" He asked as he helped pull some of the items from her to lay it on the counter.

"Bacon, there is some sausage too. It needs to thaw tonight so I can fix breakfast in the morning. All the guys will be here, because I thought we could all eat together. You don't mind do you?"

She had turned to stare up at him and he saw the sparkling in her eyes. It was excitement, how could he possibly care when he saw how much this seemed to mean to her.

"No, love, I don't mind at all. Can I help with anything?" He asked, raising his hand to tuck a stray curl behind her ear.

"Oh, no, but thank you. You all have been so busy and working so hard. I just wanted to do something nice for all of you."

Wraithe bent to place a soft kiss on her forehead as he pulled her in close for a hug. "I have something for you, do you want to see?" He asked, pulling away from her and running his hands down her arms.

She turned a beaming smile on him and asked, "For me, what is it, Wraithe?"

He smiled back at her and clutched one of her hands then tugged her slightly as they began to move down the hallway to the rec room. As they got closer, he stopped and said, "Now close your eyes love." He watched as she closed her eyes and then turned and moved down the rest of the hallway.

Wraithe stopped when they neared her gift and spoke softly. "Don't peek now, give me just a minute." Then he went and pulled the white sheet off and tossed it to the side before making his way back to Aria. Wraithe stood behind her and wrapped his arms around her. "Okay, you can look now." He said, as he squeezed her just a bit, his own excitement getting the better of him.

He heard the sharp surprised intake of breath as Aria opened her eyes. She broke from his arms and stepped quickly over to her gift, running her hands down the smooth, almost mirror like surface of the grand piano. Tear filled eyes turned to stare at him and for a moment he questioned his thinking in purchasing the piano.

Before Wraithe could ask if she was alright she was rushing at him, full speed, only to throw herself into his arms. Aria hugged him tightly. No one, since her parents, had ever given her a gift that meant so much. Tears fell to her cheeks as she held onto him.

Raising his arms and pulling her in close, Wraithe hugged her back, bending to kiss the top of her head. Waves of love, surprise, and joy poured from his little mate.

She pulled back slightly and looked up at him. Aria stared up into those beautiful golden eyes before whispering, "I love you."

It was only a few nights ago that she had told him about her piano. How she and her mother had sat for hours, laughing as she had learned to play. The proud tears that her father had shed the first time she had played by herself. How it had become their ritual, each night after dinner, her parents had sat and listened to her play. Afterward their clapping and praise for her talent would fill the room.

That was when they would share stories with her. Ones like when they had met and fell in love, that spark she would see in their eyes, as they looked at each other so lovingly during the story. The story about the night she was born and the reason they had named her Aria. Her father told her how the wind had blown so hard that night, roaring like an angry lion. He had told her about how the wind had calmed once she took her first breath and let out her first cry. And how that roaring lion had softened, the sound becoming like a soothing music, an Aria.

She told Wraithe, about the ten year old little girl whose parents didn't come home one night, and how she had sat and played the piano for them. Asking the wind to carry her playing to them, in case they were lost and needed to find their way home. Then she shared how her beautiful piano had been taken away.

Aria went to sit at the keys, she had not played since that night, but just like falling off a bike she climbed back on, and her fingers began to softly fall over the ebony and ivory.

"I didn't forget mama." She spoke so quietly, Wraithe knew it was his wolf's hearing that picked up the words.

Wraithe went and sat on one of the overstuffed chairs, content to listen as Aria played. She was lost in her memories but he didn't feel sorrow from her, only a growing sense of peace. She was saying goodbye. And as he listened to the mournful sounds he glanced outside and watched as the wind joined in on her journey. The trees swaying softly as the lightly falling snow seemed to dance. Each snow flake like a tiny dancing and swirling ballerina.

It wasn't long before he heard the mournful sounds in the distance, the wolves lending their voices to the farewell.

When the last note was played, Wraithe watched as just the slightest smile lifted the corners of her mouth. She stood and walked to him, then climbed into his lap to snuggle her body against his.

"That was beautiful my love."

Aria raised slightly and then lifted herself to press her lips against his. Wraithe wrapped his arms around her, raising one hand to curl into her hair and press her mouth closer to his. She moaned softly as she touched her tongue to his lips and he opened to let her in. The kiss deepened as their tongues met and played against each other. She reached her arms up to curl around his neck as her hands found his hair and grabbed hold pulling him closer.

Wraithe used his other hand to find the hem of her sweater then reached underneath to leave a soft trail along her skin until he found her breast. His hand danced lightly over the lacey edges of her bra while his thumb found her nipple and gently rubbed over it. She arched against him pushing her breast firmly against his palm.

Breaking the kiss Aria pulled her legs up to rest one on each side of his hips before reaching down and pulling her sweater over her head. Placing both of her hands on the top of his hands she clutched them lightly, tugging them up to place one on each breast.

She arched again into his palms and Wraithe squeezed the fullness, his thumbs lightly tracing her nipples. It didn't take long before he reached around and unhooked her bra, removing it and dropping it to the floor. He couldn't stop the hunger he felt at the sight before him. The urgent need he felt to kiss her nipples. He licked and sucked on each before finally settling on one and sucking it deeply in his mouth while his other hand molded around the opposite breast.

Aria's arms wrapped around his head and pulled his mouth closer to her breast, urging him to suck deeper. Her soft moans becoming more urgent. Wraithe's free hand found the top of her jeans and unbuttoned, then unzipped them so they lay loosely around her hips. Using his thumb on the outside he pressed hard against them where her clit should be. Her indrawn breath the only sound she made as her lower body pushed back against his thumb. The need to feel the pressure again on that pleasure spot had her hips moving back and forth, rubbing, and pressing to get closer.

Wraithe dropped his hand from her breast and wrapped it around her lower back so he could slide his hand underneath her jeans and begin working them down. As his hand slid down her ass he couldn't resist using his thumb to press gently against the little rosebud pucker. Aria moaned loudly as she sought more, he could feel the overwhelming need rising in her and if he didn't open his jeans soon his cock was going to split his jeans.

Like she had heard him, Aria reached down and opened his jeans. Once the zipper was down his cock sprang forward like a jack in the box. There was a party going on that it planned to be a part of. It was, Wraithe's turn to groan as he felt Aria's small hand wrap around him and pull up on him. Her hands so soft, it was like being wrapped in satin.

Grabbing her tightly, Wraithe stood and then lowered his head to kiss her. As the kiss deepened it became urgent and overwhelming. He had to think before he could remember why he had stood up. Remembering, he made quick work of their clothing before turning Aria and sitting her in the chair. He pushed her back against the cushions as his hands lowered to pull her hips near the edge of the chair. Then taking each leg he lifted it to rest on the edge.

Without a second thought he dove at her sweet spot, lapping and kissing. Her cries growing louder, her hands moving and threading in his hair to pull his face tighter against her. Lifting his hand he pushed one of his fingers hard into her as his lips closed around her clit and began to suck, tickling it with his tongue.

"Wraithe, oh God, Wraithe, I'm, I'm............." she cried, unable to say more, lost in the climb for ecstasy.

Wraithe removed his index finger and replaced it with his thumb. It began moving hard, in and out of her, her hips rising to take more. Then he pressed the finger that had been inside her against her sweet ass. A sharp breath was all she had time for before he was pressing it inside as well. His tongue now pressing against her clit as his fingers moved faster and harder, in and out, in and out.

He could feel the growing release that was quickly approaching for her and as her pleasure rose his tongue tickled and teased until finally she was screaming her pleasure. The sweet rain of her pussy drenching his finger.

Wraithe raised and then drove his hard stiff cock into her. He watched as the pleasure on her face increased and her hips rose to meet his as he drove into her. He couldn't hold back his own groans as her sweet body clamped around him. She was so tight inside that as he pulled out it was like being sucked back in by a vacuum.

They were in a magnificent frenzy, each of their hands moving everywhere on each other, unable to stop in just one place.

Wraithe's lips began to suckle her lower lip, one hand moving to pinch her nipple, he was too close and he knew he couldn't hold back his release from her much longer. Breaking the kiss he stared into the eyes of his mate. "Aria, come for me, my love." As he watched her eyes began to glow and the green became more brilliant than an emerald. "Your eyes, little one, they are glowing."

"So are yours, liquid amber, ohhh…Wraithe." She wailed as her release swept through her. Aria felt her fangs drop from her gums, then without a second thought she sank them deeply into Wraithe's shoulder. The first sweet taste of his blood bursting into her mouth, surging through her body and sweeping her into yet another release.

"Arrgh, oh God, Aria." Wraithe groaned as drove even deeper into her body. Sinking his fangs into her neck as well. Joining his release with hers, unable to hold back from the maelstrom of pleasure surrounding them both.

Wraithe caught his breath quickly then leaned down to nuzzle and lick her neck. Then he gently wrapped his arms around her before he stood. He headed for their bedroom, his body quivering slightly as his mate licked her mark. After placing her in the bed and grabbing the quilt to pull it over them, Wraithe pulled her close.

Inside his head, Wraithe's beast seemed to be just a little too satisfied. If it were even possible with a muzzle, he could swear that was a "shit eating grin" if he had ever seen one. What now, he wondered.

"Wraithe, thank you again, for the piano. I wish there was something I could get for you."

"You, love, I just need you."

Aria climbed up a little higher on his chest, placing a soft kiss in the center. "Does your neck hurt, I don't know what came over me."

Wraithe smiled. "Little love, you can bite me any time, it was perfect."

Chapter 14

Aria was just placing the last platter of biscuits on the large table in the rec area when the pack began arriving. She had hated leaving the warmth of Wraithe's body but she was excited about fixing breakfast for the pack, her pack, her wolf reminded her.

She didn't know what to do, how to respond to them, as they each entered and then placed their hand over their heart, nodding their head at her before taking their seat, then wishing her a good morning. She would have to ask, Wraithe, who was stoking the fire in the fireplace right now. More snow had fallen during the night, the temperature also dropping and since the rec room was so large it had a chill to it this morning.

Warm arms wrapped around her from behind and Wraithe lowered his head to nuzzle her neck. Aria smiled as she leaned back against her mate, feeling so much love and warmth pouring over her. Wraithe moved to take her hand and then led her to the head of the table, he sat her in the chair to his left before taking his seat. Reaper sat on, Wraithe's right and then Snow sat to her left, with Hawk sitting next to Reaper. Luca, Doc, and Thumper, taking the remaining seats.

Her wolf whined, then laid down, resting her head on her forelegs. *"Family."* Aria agreed, this was her family now.

The pack had all quieted as she and Wraithe took their seats. "Welcome everyone, Aria and I are glad that you could be here with us this morning. To tell you the truth, it really is nice having you here. Aria, is there anything you want to say?"

Smiling Aria glanced around the table, briefly taking in the faces of each man. "Thank you all for coming, I just wanted to tell you that I appreciate all of you watching over me and letting me get to know you. I also would like it if this could be an everyday thing. My wolf wants to be part of her pack." Aria, glancing at, Wraithe, looked for his approval and she felt very pleased when he nodded his head.

"Well guys, what do you think?" Wraithe, asked as he looked around the table.

Voices and nods of approval flowed around the table, Aria's wolf spun around and yipped in excitement.

Everyone began filling their plates and they also made sure that Aria had plenty on her plate as well. She had been an only child but now she had a room full of big brothers.

"I like the sound of that little sister." Snow replied, smiling as he turned to face her.

Aria's eyelids raised and her brows lifted, looking a lot like an owl as she starred back at Snow. She had never noticed before but his brown eyes seemed to dance with specks of copper. "You heard that, I didn't realize I had spoken out loud."

Snow shook his head and then smiled at her. "You didn't speak it out loud. I think you now have a link to us. Brothers, did all of you hear Aria speak across the link?"

Once more they all nodded in agreement.

Aria's skin tingled, she was picking up strange feelings. They were all jumbled and she had no idea what was happening to her. Laying her fork on her plate she took deep breaths trying to calm the feelings and sort through them. In her mind her wolf sat with her nose raised, as if she were scenting the air. Then lowering her head Aria noticed her glowing green eyes, her own feeling slightly warm.

Wraithe reached over to place his hand on her arm, a worried look on his face. "Aria, are you alright?" When she looked up at him he saw her eyes and they were glowing, sparking as if the emerald had caught its reflection from the fire, the same as when they had made love. "Aria?"

As she starred at, Wraithe, and took her calming breaths she realized it was the pack she was feeling. Her wolf was sorting those feelings and placing them with the pack member they belonged to. Alrighty then, so now she could feel the pack.

She raised her hand asking, Wraithe to hold on a minute. As her wolf sorted through the emotions the tingling Aria had felt started to lessen, not only did she now know who felt what, she could also feel their wolves. It was overwhelming at first but as it eased she could feel her eyes return to normal.

"Wow, that was just, wow! I don't really know how to explain it, except to say I guess my wolf was opening herself up to the pack."

Thumper was the first to speak, glancing down the table to, Wraithe. "She calmed my wolf down, he was excited or anxious I guess is the word I'm looking for. Now he is laying there, calm and still."

Murmurs of agreement went around the table, all of them looking toward, Aria.

"It's not just that, I can feel your wolves now. I have been around all of you several times in the last few days and this hasn't happened. I wonder why it happened now."

"Maybe, your wolf is just getting stronger. Ever since I met you, I have felt calm around you. Perhaps that is just another gift of yours, to bring comfort." Wraithe said, smiling as he once again reached out to take her hand.

Smiling that brilliant smile, Aria nodded her head. "Okay, I guess that sounds right, I *am* new to this after all. Alright everyone, eat up before it gets cold."

∞

It was all working out, it was actually a little better than Blackie had thought it would be. This round of demons was much more suited to the task, and they seemed to fit well with the mercs he had brought in.

Most were still here in camp but he had two that were already in a little town not far from here, Elk City. They had started by bringing the Sheriff and one of his deputies out to the camp. Now those two also carried demons. Best of all, Wraithe, was none the wiser. He didn't have a clue what was going on right under his own nose.

Blackie was expecting a larger group of the town folk this evening, yes, everything was going as planned. So why did he have this feeling that something was off? In his wolf form he had snooped around the boundaries, even crossed one to see if he could get a better look at what was going on with, Wraithe's team.

There was a new wolf with them, a snowy white female and his wolf had wanted her, badly. When, and why, had a new wolf been made, and what were her skills? He had followed up with his inside contacts and according to them a woman hadn't been turned. So where had this one come from and how?

He had definitely picked up, Wraithe's scent on her, so he was banging the help, huh? Women, they were good for one thing and that was taking his dick, hard and rough, and liking it. Other than that, he had no use for them. Speaking of that, there was a cute little waitress in town, barely eighteen if she was a day, and ripe for the picking. Yeah, he was going to be getting some of that real soon.

Getting his hands on, Wraithe's piece would be just fine too. He hadn't been able to get close enough to see her in human form, but what the hell, looks didn't matter. The look on, Wraithe's face, when he got her back, well what was left of her, now that was what mattered.

Finding a way to get her was the hard part. He didn't want to give his hand away too soon and someone was always with her. He had stayed downwind of her, trying to follow and see how close he could get, but then the wind had shifted and not only had he lost her scent, but the wind had blown all her tracks away. He still couldn't figure that one out, the snow was fresh so imprints couldn't have been covered that quickly, but they had been.

An approaching vehicle coming up the road broke into Blackie's thoughts. The sheriff's big suburban was pulling in, and he was supposed to have the mayor of Elk City with him. He was surprised that they even had a mayor, the guy was probably a barber or something like that, doubling as the mayor.

Time to take care of business. Checking back on the new wolf at, Wraithe's, camp would have to wait.

∞

"Wraithe, someone was out in the woods today. I couldn't really pick up the scent, he stayed downwind of us and I didn't want to leave Aria to go have a look. Wraithe, my wolf was very agitated, I've never seen him like this. Thumper whispered, trying to keep his voice down so Aria wouldn't hear, he didn't want to scare her.

Wraithe motioned for, Thumper, to step outside with him. "Did you maybe just come across someone that was curious, maybe just wanting to see the wolves? It couldn't have been a hunter, the wolves up here are protected."

"I'm not sure, but we were definitely being followed. Besides, what person in their right mind would be stupid enough to follow wolves?"

"We haven't had anyone check in with us, one of the scientists that come to check up on the natural wolves?"

"I thought of that, and checked with Doc to see if that was a possibility, but no, he hasn't had any word about someone being here."

"You don't think, Aria, picked up on any of this?"

"No, I don't think so, but it's hard to tell with her sometimes. Wraithe, the wind, it knew something was wrong. When I started moving, Aria, back to camp, I looked back and it was covering our tracks with snow. I was right beside, Aria, and I couldn't pick up her scent, couldn't pick up my own for that matter."

"It will be dark soon, get with, Snow, tell him what's going on. He and, Hawk have the perimeter tonight, and they are damn good trackers. See what they can find, and, Thumper, I don't care what time it is, I want to know what they find."

Thumper took off down the steps as, Wraithe stepped back inside. Aria, was talking to, Zeus, as she prepared dinner. It smelled like beef stew, that would certainly hit the spot, his wolf whined, guess he was hungry too.

Aria looked up at, Wraithe, when he seated himself at the counter. "Wraithe, did, Thumper, tell you that we were followed today?"

Smiling at his beautiful little mate, Wraithe thought, yeah, no getting anything over on her.

"Yes, he did tell me. Did your wolf pick up on someone?"

"Yeah, she did, she could sense him, not smell him. She did *not* like him. The wind warned me too, I had it cover our tracks and it was already removing our scents. Who do you think it was, Wraithe?"

"I'm not sure, love, but, Snow, and, Hawk, will be checking out the area tonight. Aria, you know what's going on out there, I want you to be careful. Stay close to the cabin, okay, can you do that for me?"

Aria walked around the counter and as, Wraithe swiveled his seat around she pushed between his thighs to snuggle against his chest. She had discovered it was her most favorite place in the world, being snuggled up against him.

Wraithe wrapped his arms around her and nuzzled her neck. He had always loved her scent, but now that it was combined with his he was drawn to her even more. It still amazed him how quickly they had bonded, how easily they had come to love each other. He had never imagined his life with someone in it, at least not in the long term. Now, he couldn't imagine his life without her, nothing mattered more to him. He would protect her until his last breath, because without her there would be nothing left, he would be an empty shell.

His hold on her tightened, his thoughts having drifted to a place where he refused to go. He had taken every precaution that he could to insure her safety.

"Wraithe, do you think that the person in the woods might have something to do with the portal? What about the portal, you haven't mentioned if there has been any luck finding it." Aria asked, pulling back from him slightly so she could look up into his face.

"I'm not sure, love, but it is a possibility. That is why I want you to be careful. We've been scouting the area around where you were camping. You said that your friends went for a hike, while you were resting, right?" Wraithe watched as, Aria, nodded her head.

"So we have been branching out in a circle around that area, covering a distance that we thought they might have hiked. We think a general direction of the portal has been found, our wolves become more alert, more anxious when we are near that particular area."

Aria starred at, Wraithe, then asked a question she had been dreading. "You're going to go in there, aren't you?"

Wraithe watched as tears gathered in those big green eyes, it tore at his heart to see her sad. "Aria, love, I have to, but you know what?" He asked, watching as her cute little brow rose in question. She really did have a very expressive face.

"Aria, have you forgotten the beast I carry in me? Do you think he would ever let anything happen to me?"

"No, you're right, my warrior would never let you be taken from me." Once more she snuggled back against his chest.

Wraithe rested his head against the top of her head and turned his thoughts inward. *"You hear that, beast, she trusts you, don't let her down."* Wraithe smiled when the beast growled at him, then he purred, Aria snuggling in even closer to the sound. *"Will never let little one down."*

"My love, how does a trip into town with me sound for tomorrow morning? Elk City is a nice little mountain town. It has this old fashioned diner, fountain drinks and all, and they make the best chocolate shakes, how does that sound?"

"Wraithe, it sounds perfect, yes I would love to go. Chocolate shakes, you said, hum, yep, that would make the trip worth it."

"And here I thought being with me would make the trip worth it."

Aria giggled then raised to her tip toes to place a tender kiss on his lips. "Oh, you are, but chocolate shakes, well they are a bonus."

Wraithe stood and then lifted her up his body and when she wrapped her legs around his waist he asked. "How long till dinner?" Turning, he headed toward the hall and the bedroom.

"About an hour, why, did you have something you needed to do?" Aria asked, giggling as his hands reached down to hold her by her butt cheeks.

"Oh yeah, I have something I need to take care of right away, and that is just enough time for me to do it correctly."

Wraithe nuzzled her neck and she swung her head to get her hair out of the way. He went directly for his mark on her neck, and began licking it with his tongue, sending shivers through her body.

"Hum, yes, well it's always best if you can get it right, the first time."

Chapter 15

Elk City was a beautiful little town, with one main street being the concourse of business and activity. Each building painted a different color, but done tastefully to blend and accent each other. The town hall was at one end with a small white church at the opposite end. Aria thought the best way to describe it was, adorably charming.

She and, Wraithe, had walked down one side of the street, slipping inside, craft shops, clothing shops, and an antique shop before reaching the General Store.

Aria felt like she had stepped back in time, bolts of cloth on shelves built into the wall, sewing adornments on tables nearby. There were even glass jars of candy sitting at the front counter. Rows of food stock were at one side of the store and tables with clothing folded neatly on top were placed to the opposite side. There was a catalog sitting on a tall counter, a chair pulled up in front of it, but she discovered modern technology had made its way here as well. Sitting next to the catalog was a computer with a small sign "place orders", sitting next to it.

Aria began to move back toward the front, noticing that, Wraithe, was finishing his business. As she passed the large glass pane that looked out on the street she noticed the small table with a chair sitting on each end, a checker board and checkers sitting on top. There was something so serene about this setting, it brought back another time, when life moved at a simpler pace.

Wraithe startled her from her thoughts asking, "Care for a game?"

Laughing as she swatted his arm for startling her, she said. "No, but I could sure go for that milk shake you were talking about last night."

Reaching down, Wraithe took her hand to place in the crook of his arm before heading them toward the door.

They entered the diner laughing, and Wraithe led her to a seat at the fountain counter. While he placed their order for burgers and shakes, Aria looked around the diner.

There were older black and white photos, and current color pictures hung on all the walls. Booths lined the walls with tables and chairs making up the remainder of the seating. The floor was a black and white polished linoleum but it wasn't as worn as she would've expected. Although it had the older feel, the place had been loved and well cared for. Repairs and updates made when needed.

Aria thought that at one time she would have loved to call a town like this home. The people were friendly and offered warm smiles and greetings. It was a beautiful community and she was glad, Wraithe had brought her along.

The young woman behind the counter that was waiting on them had the sweetest smile. She was friendly, and polite, but not over talkative. Aria thought she must be either a senior in high school or she had graduated this past spring. She had long thick black hair, even pulled into a ponytail it hung to her hips, and she had the bluest eyes, Aria, had ever seen. She had introduced herself as Luna, Aria thought it suited her, her pale skin looked like it would glow in the moonlight.

Aria wasn't sure why, but she felt drawn to the young woman, her wolf agreeing as she whined and sniffed at the air. There was something about her and Aria had a feeling she would be seeing the young woman again.

With their meal finished and to go cups filled with the remainder of their shakes, Wraithe, and Aria, headed back to the SUV. As they were buckling themselves in the Sheriff's suburban pulled in to park beside them.

Wraithe started their vehicle as the sheriff walked in front. He tipped his hat and starred at Aria, smiling as he continued on his way.

Aria drew in a sharp breath, reaching over to grab, Wraithe's arm. "Wraithe, he is one of them, did you see his eyes?"

Wraithe looked out the window to watch the sheriff, only getting a view of his back. He hadn't seen his eyes, but if Aria said it was one of those things then he knew it was. Wraithe rolled down his window and took a deep breath, both of his wolves began to growl and snarl in his head. The beast trying to come forward. This was not the time, he thought. Aria, was with him, she would be alone if he went to find the sheriff and he hadn't brought his sword.

This would have to be handled in a different way he told his wolves, they calmed but remained on alert, ready to protect their mate. Wraithe, couldn't get her out of there fast enough, quickly putting the SUV in reverse and backing out, then heading out of town, getting some distance between her and that thing as quickly as possible.

They were a few miles outside of town when, Aria groaned. "Wraithe, my wolf, she wants out, I can't….stop her."

Wraithe immediately began sending calming feelings to his mate, the alpha in him standing up to her. Growling across their link to his mate to calm.

"Deep breaths, Aria, take deep breaths."

Her claws had lengthened from the tips of her fingers, her eyes having changed, not glowing this time but becoming that deeper green. He watched as she took the slow deep breaths. Glancing between her and the road he finally noticed the tension in her body begin to relax. She had done it, her wolf was letting go.

"Aria, love, are you okay?" Concern for her clearly noticeable in his dulcet tones.

"Yeah, yeah, I'm fine now, thank you. It was a little scary there for a minute."

"I hate to use the old cliché, 'been there, done that', but it has happened to us all, Aria. You actually did pretty well, the first time it happened to me my hair had sprouted before I could call my wolf back."

"If your wolf hadn't stopped her, I probably would have changed, she wasn't listening to me. He deserves a good belly rub." She said as she turned her laughing smile on him.

Reaching over, Wraithe squeezed her thigh. "I think he might have a better idea in mind." Wraithe wiggled his eyebrows up and down. Rewarded for his efforts by her beautiful laugh.

They made it back to the cabins in no time at all. Wraithe helped, Aria, out of the truck assuring her he would join her shortly. He had already sent a message to the pack over their link, and by time he arrived at the smaller practice clearing they were waiting.

Wraithe looked at the faces starring back at him. They were ready, hardened warriors stood before him, each with their own special skill set. They weren't going on their first mission, it didn't matter that the paradigm had shifted, what they were fighting for hadn't.

"It's begun." Wraithe spoke as he looked to each man. "As, Aria, and I were leaving town we saw the Sheriff, he is changed. He let his eyes show when he looked at, Aria, and then I got a whiff of him. You'll know the scent when you smell it, there is no missing it. I'm not sure how many of the people in Elk City are compromised. We need to start with recon and where possible take out the ones we can. We don't want to start a panic with the townspeople so if you can't do it without witnesses, let them go."

Reaper spoke up. "Their eyes take on a mirror like shine, well it's more like a cat's eyes when light hits them a certain way."

Wraithe nodded his agreement. "Yeah, but if they are in town I don't imagine their eyes are always like that. People would notice. I think they can conceal their eyes, either not showing them unless they want or only when the demon is closer to the surface, like with our wolves. The scent of those things is always present, but not something that a normal person would smell. So use their scent to locate them, and when you can't take them out, watch them. We might get lucky, and one of them lead us back to that portal."

"Reaper, I want you and, Luca, to go into town. Snoop around a bit, you know the drill. Song, you and, Hawk, I want the two of you with them, but in wolf form on the outskirts of town. Take your swords, and be careful."

"Doc, you and, Thumper, gather whatever you think you will need and meet back at my cabin. I want everyone staying there going forward. Any questions?"

"Alright, let's do this." Wraithe said, watching as they moved to carry out his orders. The twins hadn't found anything other than the recent scent of a new wolf, not one of their pack, the night before, had it been following, Aria, and, Thumper, looking for a pack to join? He needed to be on the lookout.

One thing kept bothering him about that Sheriff, why had it showed its eyes to Aria? Do they know about her somehow, or had it shown its eyes by accident? Wraithe didn't believe in that type of mistake, especially when he was going up against an enemy that was new to him.

He opened his link with her, she was just getting out of the shower, she was safe. Still he picked up speed, reaching the cabin quickly and taking the steps two at a time. Aria, was still dressing so, Wraithe took the time to move around the cabin, locking things up tight. He had just finished when, Doc, and, Thumper arrived.

"Hey, guys, come on in. Make yourself at home. Doc, the rec area will be the best place to set up your supplies."

Doc looked around the room and not seeing, Aria, he replied. "At some point I thought we would all end up here so I have already stored medical supplies back there. We heal pretty quickly, but I have everything here that I might need."

"Thanks, Doc. Okay, both of you get your gear put away upstairs. Dinner will be ready in a bit."

Aria, was just heading into the kitchen when, Thumper, and Doc reached the stairs. "Hi, Thumper, Doc. How are you tonight?" She asked, smiling while she started pulling pans from the cabinets. "Will you be joining us for dinner?"

"Ah, Aria, we're fine, you look lovely as ever." Doc, said while, Thumper stood smiling beside him. "Wraithe, wants us here for a few days, I hope it won't be an imposition. I certainly won't mind having your cooking over my own."

Aria's smile went from soft to brilliant. "Of course it's not an imposition, I love having you here. Please, make yourself at home, dinner will be ready soon. Hope you like steak."

"Oh yeah, that sounds good. I will be back down in a few, lend you a hand if you need it." Thumper said while making his way up the stairs, Doc, following behind.

Wraithe, wrapped his arms around, Aria, and pulled her against him. He lowered his lips to hers for a soft kiss. "Mmm, you taste good, how about we let them fix their own dinner and I eat you for dinner?"

Aria, laughed and lightly slapped, Wraithe's chest. "Oh you are incorrigible. Now be a good boy and go start the grill, please."

Chapter 16

So far, Reaper wasn't happy about anything they were finding. The Sheriff, one of his deputies and apparently the mayor were all carrying that demon in them. They had picked up on two others, but from what, Reaper could tell they weren't residents here.

Right now it was best just to follow them, see what they were up to. Reaper didn't like it, something about the way they moved, the way they acted and looked. They were soldiers, at least at one time they had been. They didn't act like they were active, there was a certain way an active duty soldier comported themselves, even out of uniform.

"Shit!" He thought, out loud, 'they're mercs.' He looked over at Luca as they continued to walk toward the diner. Luca whistled a low release of breath. Reaper opened the link and told the twins, and then closed the link.

Entering the diner, Reaper, and, Luca seated themselves in a booth, closest to the front door. The corner booth was a half circle, which was in their favor because you never wanted a door at your back. Grabbing some menus that sat in the middle of the table they opened them up, pretending to be deciding on a meal.

The mercs sat at a table further down and were also looking at menus. The young waitress came from behind the counter carrying a tray with four glasses of ice water. She sat two down at the mercs table, telling them she would be right back and headed toward, Reaper, and, Luca.

Setting the glasses down on their table, she introduced herself. "Hi, I'm Luna, can I get you something else to drink?"

"Coffee would be great, thanks Luna." Luca replied, taking the opportunity to look down at the mercs.

"Sure, I'll be right back."

Luna made her way back and took a drink order from the mercs as well before heading back around the counter.

Luca, and, Reaper, tuned their wolf hearing into the conversation the mercs were having.

"There will be four to take back tonight. The remaining three deputies, and the boss wants that pretty little thing over there behind the counter." The bigger of the two mercs whispered. "We get her when he is through with her, bet she will be a good ride." He said, laughing quietly, but stopped as Luna approached carrying their sodas. She sat them down then walked back over to the booth.

Reaper, and, Luca, both had to rein in their wolves. They were howling mad and snapping their jaws. Luna sat their coffee down before stepping back slightly.

"Would you like to order something to eat, the grill is going to close soon so if you want a burger I need to turn in the order."

Luca thought she was a sweet kid, and no way in hell were those things getting her. "Yeah, I will take one, fully loaded with fries, please." He said, watching as she smiled and wrote down his order before turning to Reaper.

"Sounds good, I'll have the same, thanks. What time do you close?"

"In a little less than an hour. Two burgers with fries, coming up."

Luca watched as she made her way back to the demons. They ordered the burgers too, and smiling, Luna told them they would be up shortly, and then moved back behind the counter.

Reaper opened the link with the twins, telling them what was going on. Then he told them to be at the diner within half an hour but to remain hidden.

Speaking across their link, Reaper, and, Luca discussed a plan. They would stick with the two mercs, and the twins would follow

Luna home. Snow, and, Hawk, would stay close to her until Reaper gave them the all clear. This plan hinged on the mercs not knowing where she lived. Chances were they had been told to retrieve her after the diner closed, at least that is what they hoped.

A short time later it was all a moot point, the door to the diner opened, allowing a slight breeze to drift through along with the newest patron.

Luca watched as both mercs took in deep breaths, each turning their heads to look over at Luca, and, Reaper. Their eyes flashed that mirror like black and in an instant it was gone, the eyes back to normal.

Luna was about to step from behind the counter with their meals when both stood, and threw some money on the table. Keeping a close eye on Luca, and, Reaper, they started for the door to leave.

"Hey, don't you want your burgers?" She called after them, a slightly stunned look on her face.

"Something came up." One of them called back to her and then like that they made their exit and were gone.

"Luna, if you don't mind, we'll take ours to go." Luca called over to her.

"Yeah, sure, no problem. Is everything okay, did I offend someone or something?" She asked, still looking a little confused by what had just happened.

"Nah, honey, you didn't do anything wrong, time just got away from us and we have to get back." Luca replied.

"Alright, give me just a minute and I will get these packed up for you." She said, while turning to go back behind the counter again.

"Luca, the twins are going to stick close, and they will follow her home as planned."

Luca nodded. "Is it just me Reaper, or did you get the feeling those guys recognized our scents?"

"I don't know if they recognized them, but they definitely knew we were wolves."

Reaper turned, hearing Luna approaching and went quiet.

Luca handed her a couple of twenties and asked. "Will that cover it?"

"Yeah, but one twenty will do it."

"That's okay, you keep the change. Thanks Luna, have a nice evening, you be safe now."

"Thank you, I will, come again." She said, smiling brightly back at Luca.

"Goodnight." Luca replied, while he and Reaper made their way to the door, exiting the diner.

Following the mercs scent they headed up toward the small courthouse which sat at the edge of town. Fortunately the SUV was parked just a block up and once they reached it they climbed in. With the tinted windows it was less likely they would be noticed. Now it was time to watch, and wait.

They weren't the only ones watching, Luca thought to himself. A large owl sat perched on the branch of a tree that was a couple of doors down from the SUV. That was a little odd, it was a large owl, and although he couldn't recall what kind it was, he knew it wasn't normal for one to be seen this close to a town much less be in one.

∞

Wraithe couldn't shake this nagging feeling that something was wrong and both of his wolves were in agreement. He had decided to send, Doc, and, Thumper out to run the night boundary but because he couldn't shake this sense that something was wrong he was going with them. It was against his better judgment, but he couldn't leave, Aria, here alone so she was coming with them.

Wraithe and the guys stripped outside, donning their swords before shifting, and then waited for, Aria. They didn't have to wait long, with, Zeus, on her heels, Aria, joined them. She was still shy when it came to stripping in front of the rest of the pack and in all honesty, Wraithe was pleased by that. He didn't know how he would react if they saw that beautiful body he considered to be his, but there was no reason to push the matter either.

Turning his nose to the air, Wraithe breathed in deep, deciding on a direction he headed out. Aria, at his side, Zeus, Doc, and Thumper bringing up the rear. They crossed the clearing where they practiced and headed toward the lake. A light snow that had fallen earlier lay like dust on top of the leaves and some of the fallen branches and logs.

They hadn't gone far when Wraithe picked up the scent of blood and wolf, his wolf growling as he picked up speed. As the scent grew heavier he realized it was the scent of a couple of the natural wolves in his pack, and it was their blood he smelled. He also picked up the scent of another wolf, one he didn't recognize and without thought the beast had come out, running, sword in hand. He might have become the alpha in unfortunate ways but he was still their alpha, it was his responsibility to protect them. Reaching the wolves much quicker, thanks to the speed of his beast, Wraithe starred around in shock at what he found.

Two male wolves, they had been ripped to pieces, body parts thrown in several different directions. Butchered, the crimson of their blood coating the ground all around him. It looked all the more brutal because of the snow. Wraithe's beast snarled before letting out a blood curdling howl that was like nothing, Wraithe had ever heard or even known he was capable of. Not only was it a warning of danger, but one of pure sorrow, Wraithe realized. He was overwhelmed with helplessness and anger at the senseless slaughter that lay before him.

Before he could think to send word to, Doc, and, Thumper to stop, Aria from coming in, he heard her whine behind him. He turned to look at her, her heart was breaking and there was no comfort he could offer her, not for this.

The alpha female starred around her at the carnage, and whined. She moved to the head of each wolf, sniffed, and then ran her face against theirs. Her beautiful snowy white face marked with their blood. She moved to sit between the two, then raising her head, she too howled her song of grief, joined by, Doc, and, Thumper.

In the distance, Wraithe could hear the response not only from the direction of the cave where his natural wolf pack denned, but from the opposite direction, the other natural wolf pack. All joined together in sadness and loss.

"Evil one did this." The beast whispered softly in, Wraithe's head. *"You mean a demon has possessed a wolf?"* Wraithe asked. *"Yes."* Wraithe breathed in the scents around him, and there it was. Not as heavy as when they were in a human, but a demon just the same.

Several miles away Blackie, in his wolf form stopped and listened. His wolf tensed when it heard that first howl and turned back to look in the direction they had come from. 'Wraithe, has found my little gift, has he?' He thought to himself, and laughed. "The first of many my old friend, the first of many." Then hearing the wolves howling in all directions around him, Blackie headed back to camp, his beast moving a little faster this time.

Chapter 17

Snow, and, Hawk perked up their ears, the wind carrying the sounds of pain and loss. It was their alpha female, and her sorrow was being carried across the night skies. Their wolves tried desperately to join her call, but they were in town, watching over the young woman, Luna. The twins tried to reach out over their link but they were too far away. Remaining in the shadows they moved closer together, whining as they rubbed against the other to offer comfort.

A door opened at the back of the house, Luna stepping out onto the porch. Cocking her head she listened, and as the twins watched from the darkness tears began to fall on her face. Wrapping her arms around herself she sat down on the porch step, rocking back and forth.

She shouldn't have been able to hear the wolves in the distance but she had. Snow stepped closer to get a better look at the young woman, but he made sure to remain in the cover of trees.

"I know you're there, I'm sorry for your loss. I pray the great spirits bring you comfort." With that she stood and walked back to the porch door, looking back once to scan the trees where, Snow, and, Hawk stood, she bowed her head. "Peace, brother wolf." With that she stepped inside and closed the door leaving the twins to wonder at this strange young woman.

A few miles away, Reaper, and, Luca closed the link opened by the twins. They were puzzled as well by the strange events they'd just been shown. Several times, Reaper had tried to call, Wraithe, and the others, but there was no answer. Both of them had felt the sorrow coming from, Aria, and as badly as they hated not being able to go to her there was nothing to be done.

It was getting late, almost midnight and nothing had happened. Then again maybe that was about to change as, Reaper watched the light breaking onto the sidewalk from a door opening at the jail. A moment later the sheriff's suburban drove up in front, not pulling into a parking place, just pulling up near the curb.

Reaper started his SUV and continued to watch as the Sheriff stepped from his vehicle just as the two mercs were stepping out of the door. They each carried the body of a deputy thrown over their shoulders. While they opened the passenger doors on the suburban another deputy stepped from the jail. He was also carrying a body, the third deputy, who he tossed into the very back of the waiting car.

They needed to stop them, if not then the fate of those deputies would be sealed and demons would possess them as well. If they interfered then the possibility of the demons all being killed was high, while finding that portal was low. Not to mention dealing with the fallout if the sheriff and deputy went missing. All they could do at this point was follow and watch. Hope that another opportunity would present itself to rescue the deputies.

The sheriff and deputy climbed into the suburban and pulled away, heading out of town while the two mercs got into another dark SUV. Backing out of their parking place they went a different direction.

As, Reaper watched they turned a corner and were out of sight. He backed out as quickly as he could without squealing his tires and headed out of town, following the sheriff. If those two mercs were headed for, Luna, the twins would take care of them.

Reaper raced to catch up with the sheriff's vehicle but not close enough to draw notice that they were being followed. Doing at least eighty and turning his lights off he used his wolf's vision to navigate the road and watch for the suburban. He had just caught a glimpse of taillights when they turned off the road, Reaper slowed, not wanting to draw attention by coming up to fast. He wasn't sure how well those demons could see. Reaching the turnoff he pulled past it a bit, then turned around and parked the SUV between a break in the tree line.

Looking over at, Luca, he said. "Time to wolf it."

Making quick work of their clothes and slinging on the swords they shifted. Their wolves quickly running off into the trees and following the muddy dirt road the suburban had taken. The wolves easily caught up with the vehicle, continuing to follow from within the forest.

Having traveled several miles the suburban turned again, but this time it wasn't a road although the grasses had been beaten down by the snow and a heavy vehicle or two. Slowing their pace the wolves worked their way in quietly.

"Work your way around, I'll meet you on the back side." Reaper spoke across his link, watching as Luca slid off into the night.

Reaper wasn't believing what he was seeing. Several tents had been setup, a large fire was in the center of what was a fairly large campsite. Just slightly off to the side, not far from the camp was a large grouping of rocks, mostly covered by snow but small patches of moss were visible. One side of the grouping was bare of any snow, probably due to its almost flat upright shape.

This place was all wrong, Reaper knew it and his wolf did to. As he made his way around he watched as the deputies taken from town were unloaded from the suburban. Then tossed over another merc's shoulders they were taken over to that rock face and laid out in front of it. Opening his link with, Luca, he asked. "Are you seeing this? That must be the door."

"Copy." Luca replied.

Meeting up at the back, Luca, and, Reaper lowered to their bellies and watched from the shadows. "They have some good fire power, Reaper, and some explosives. I counted ten, not including the sheriff and his deputy." Movement toward that rock face caught their attention and as they watched, several of the demons approached it.

The light color of the rock seemed to darken, becoming black. Looking at it from this vantage point it appeared more like the opening on a cave than a solid rock. Moments later three reddish things began to creep out of the black, taking a place at the head of each of the three deputies laying near the opening. The beings were bare of any hair, their bodies twisted and withered. Sharp claws protruded from overly long fingers, their mouths misshapen and full of pointed teeth on the top and bottom, the eyes lifeless, dead.

There was nothing that, Reaper, or, Luca, could do but watch. Their orders were to recon, and to make matters worse, well, there was just no way they could take all of them on and make it out of there with the deputies in tow.

The demons took on a dark shadowy appearance and then lifted the body laid out in front of them. Then just as easy as that they stepped into the body. The deputies', bodies jerked, and stretched, it literally looked like they were being tried on from the inside. While the body, or was it their souls within, that tried desperately to fight off what had climbed inside.

Luca thought he was going to be sick, and worse, his wolf was becoming more and more difficult to hold back.

"Luca, lets go, come on, we are outta here."

Slinking back deeper into the cover of the trees they moved back around the camp and headed to the SUV. The link between them remaining silent as they traveled. What was there to say after what they had witnessed? There were no words for that horror or the sick feeling that was riding in their guts. Then, most of all the anger, of not being able to save those deputies.

It didn't take long to get back to the SUV, shift and dress to get the hell out of there. "Reaper, if, if they ever get me don't....." Luca's voice breaking, unable to get the rest out he went quiet.

Reaching over, Reaper placed his hand on, Luca's shoulder then squeezed. "I'll take care of it buddy, I'll take care of it." Then he put the SUV in gear and hit the gas.

When they pulled back into town, Reaper opened the link with the twins. "You guys, okay?" He asked.

"They came for, Luna." Snow answered. "We killed both of them before they could get to close to the house. The bodies burn to ash when you take the head. Did you find the door?"

"Yeah, we'll meet you where we dropped you off. It's time to get back." Reaper wouldn't say more. The rest would have to wait till he filled, Wraithe, in on what they had seen. He was only repeating that shit once. If he had doubts about having another wolf in him, they were long gone now. Bring it, he thought.

Chapter 18

Wraithe sat on the large sofa near the fire in the front room, Aria, curled in his lap. Her eyes finally dry of tears. He was a soldier and didn't know the first thing about comforting someone. All he could do was hold her, praying it was enough.

When they had returned to the cabin she had shifted and dressed, silent tears falling from her eyes. He could feel the hurt and anger that rolled off of her like a heavy fog. She had tried to busy herself with anything she could find that would take her mind away from what had been found. Zeus faithfully following behind her or stopping at her side, pressing against her leg as if he were saying 'I'm here to lean on', and Wraithe hadn't overlooked the small reassuring pats she gave the big dog. It was late but she refused to go to bed.

Doc, and, Thumper had returned with the bodies of the wolves, building a fire in the clearing to burn them instead of allowing them to be left for scavengers.

Wraithe hadn't wanted, Aria, to be there when they set the blaze, but she felt it was her duty, she wanted to see them safely away, she had said. Holding his hand as they walked toward the pyre, she dried her tears and carried herself straight and proud.

What he hadn't expected was to see the pack of natural wolves that stood in the tree line, watching. Wraithe had ordered them to the safety of the den earlier when the dead wolves had been found.

"Wraithe, I called to them. Please, don't be angry with them. I don't know what is driving me to do this, only that this is the way it must be done." Aria had said quietly.

"No, my love, I'm not angry, do what you need to do."

A nod from Wraithe, and, Thumper lit the fire, the bodies or rather the pieces of, having already been placed on top. As the blaze took hold it lit the night sky, the smoke drifting up into the darkness overhead.

"Wind, come to me." Aria called. In only moments the wind swept around them, licking at the fire, forcing it to spread on the rest of the branches and logs, burning hotter and brighter. "Take them home." She said softly, and as they watched, the wind took the smoke and pulled it heavenward, sending it in several different directions.

Aria stepped back slightly and released, Wraithe's hand before she began to undress. Wraithe nodded to, Doc, and, Thumper, the three of them undressing as well. Together they joined, Aria, in the shift.

Silently the wolves within the tree line made their way forward, although they remained further out from the fire. They gathered behind, Aria, and Wraithe watching for what their alpha pair would do next.

Lifting her head, Aria once more howled into the night, surrounded by her pack, their howls joining hers, she released her sorrow, and said her goodbyes. When the last howl had drifted away they all had sat, and watched as the fire burned down, urged on by the wind to burn quickly.

When the flames had burnt low, leaving only the embers, the natural pack drifted away while, Aria, and, Wraithe had dressed and then made their way back to the cabin.

Once inside, Wraithe picked, Aria, up and then sat on the sofa. And here they still sat, with his mate wrapped snuggly in his arms. It was early morning, now, Aria had finally drifted to sleep just a little more than an hour ago. Unable to find sleep himself he was left with his thoughts. Those demons, what they had done, yeah, it was personal now. They had hurt his mate. It might not have been a physical injury but it was just as bad. What had been done to members of his pack was unforgivable.

Wraithe knew when Reaper and the rest returned but he had asked that they use the back stairs to go to their rooms. Reaper had the information they needed, and, Wraithe more than anyone knew it was important, but, Aria, came first, she always would. There would be time enough later to discuss it and make their plans.

∞

Aria entered the kitchen looking around for, Wraithe, but he wasn't there. She opened her link and called to him. "Wraithe, is everything okay?"

"Good morning, love, yes, everything is fine. How are you today? You really should sleep a little longer."

"I'm good handsome, I just got used to waking up with you next to me."

"I'll be back soon. Reaper and the other guys got back and I'm going over what they found out." Wraithe replied, he still felt some of the sadness across their link.

"Alright, I will get some sandwiches ready, how is that?" She asked.

"Sounds perfect, sweetheart, see you soon. Oh, before I forget, Zeus, is with me."

Aria had just finished setting everything out on the counter when the pack arrived back at the cabin. She felt relief knowing they were all home and they were all safe. There were plenty of meats, cheeses, bread and chips all ready to go, she had even whipped up a pasta salad.

What happened yesterday had hit her hard and she knew she must have seemed so weak to her pack. Everything that had happened recently came crashing back on top of her, the loss of her parents, and the loss of her friends. The social workers had felt she was too young to be at the funeral for her parents, and there would never be one for her friends. Last night she had been able to release her grief, and she hadn't realized how much of it she had been holding back.

Wraithe pulled her into his arms, kissing the top of her head. With that simple gesture she felt all the tension finally leave her body. She felt no judgment, or disappointment from him, only love.

∞

"What the hell do you mean they didn't come back, where the hell are they?" Blackie growled, barely holding on to his anger. He was furious, he'd been expecting that little waitress but what pissed him off more was the thought of his orders being disobeyed. "Mack, you find those sons of bitches and bring them back here now!"

"I'm on it." Mack replied, as he turned and left Blackie's tent.

Blackie was not about to start putting up with these fucking things not following his orders, not this early in the game. There was too much at stake for any of them to go off halfcocked. He would kill them himself if he found out the two of them had played with the little waitress before he got her. He had plans for her, hell his wolf had some plans for her too.

Mack would deal with it, he would find them. Blackie didn't have time for this today. Last night when he had stepped out of his tent to see the new deputies he could have sworn his wolf smelled other wolves nearby, and not just any wolves, they were from Wraithe's team. He had tried to pick up more of the scent last night but it was like it just disappeared, so he wasn't exactly sure he had scented them at all. He needed to shift and go have a look around.

Leaving his tent he began making his way around the camp but there was nothing. Shifting he moved off deeper into the tree line, looking for signs of someone being there instead of just scenting for them. He was about to chalk it up to paranoia when he finally noticed something. There weren't any footprints, human, or wolf, but there were some broken limbs. When he followed them back up toward the main road he found tire tracks where a heavy vehicle had sat in the snow. There was still no scent but someone had definitely been parked here.

'Shit!" They had found the camp, he thought to himself. No, he couldn't be positive that it was, Wraithe's team, but it was better to be safe than sorry. He didn't believe in coincidence.

A noise up in one of the trees caught his wolf's attention and he growled when he looked up, sniffing at the air. Sitting there just watching was a large snow white owl. His wolf tensed then snarled at the bird. Jumping at the tree trunk and digging in with his claws he quickly scaled the tree trying to reach the owl. Before he could reach his prey the owl spread its wings and took off into the sky, the sight of it lost in the clouds that hung heavy and low.

"Old one." The wolf growled out deeply.

Chapter 19

The large white owl soared through the night skies catching one wind current after another to easily glide toward his destination. Rarely having to expend any energy to flap his great wings which would propel him in flight. The clouds were heavy tonight, there were no stars or even the moon to light his way, there seldom was this time of year, not that he needed it to see by. He had delayed heading back so that he could check the warriors, satisfied with their progress he was headed home.

He needed to feed, but he had lost his appetite a long time ago. There was no flavor anymore, it had become a chore instead of a pleasure. It was only necessity, nothing more. Life itself held no meaning for him, there was no excitement, no joy, not even sadness, only the sense of duty.

Banking to the east he slowed his speed before descending onto the balcony. Smoothly shifting back into his normal form as his feet touched the floor softly and he stepped into the room. He looked to his brother who sat quietly by the fire, awaiting his return.

"It won't be long now, the dark wolf will soon know we have called the blood wolves." Wulfgar spoke as he took the seat opposite his brother, and stared into the flames.

"How long will it be brother, before the rest of the gifts begin to arrive? Time isn't on our side, he will double his efforts to take over more bodies for the dark ones."

"Another is on her way, and one has already been noticed but it wasn't by her warrior, but, I think that is about to change quickly."

"And the Guardians, when will you make the call to wake them?"

Wulfgar sighed heavily, and then looked at his brother. "Soon, we no longer have a choice."

Thumper closed the main cabin door quietly behind him as he entered. He had a surprise for, Aria, and he hoped it would lift her spirits. She actually seemed much better this evening but he wanted to see that bright happy smile back on her face. For over a week now she had been trying to figure out why they called him, Thumper so he thought it would be better if he just showed her. Wraithe had gone out with the rest of the pack to run the evening perimeter, now was the perfect time, he wouldn't have to deal with the other guys poking fun at him.

Sitting on some pillows in front of the fire, Aria sat quietly watching the flames. Slowly running her hand down the back of her big black lab that lay in front of her.

"Aria, how are you?" Thumper asked, watching as she turned her head, and stared up at him.

Smiling softly she replied quietly. "I'm fine, Thumper, how are you? The fire is nice, would you like to join me?"

"I'm good, and, yeah, that fire looks nice but I wanted to show you something, and, well, tell you something too, if you have a minute."

"Of course, Thumper, please, have a seat."

Thumper sat down cross legged on the hardwood floor then reached inside his jacket. As, Aria watched he pulled a large black and white floppy eared rabbit from inside his jacket. She took a quick indrawn breath and then clasped her hands at her mouth.

"Aria, this is Nibbles, Nibbles, this is, Aria. Would you like to hold her?" He asked, smiling brightly at, Aria, pleased very much by her reaction.

"Oh, yes, please." Aria said, reaching for the rabbit, her beautiful smile once again shining.

Thumper placed, Nibbles in, Aria's hands, then sat back to watch as she cradled the rabbit close to her chest, speaking softly to it, and making soft cooing noises.

"Oh, Thumper, she is so soft."

"Nibbles, is a French Lop Ear. She is my favorite, now don't tell anyone but I let her sleep with me." He said, speaking just above a whisper.

"She is adorable, thank you.....wait, Thumper, your name? That, is why they call you, Thumper, the rabbit?" Aria, laughed as she stared at, Thumper, waiting for his answer.

"Yeah, now you know, and it's not just rabbit, it's rabbitssss." He said, looking back at her sheepishly, just a little bit of a blush on his cheeks.

"I actually have several and believe it or not they use a litter box. I don't cage them like most people do. I have always had rabbits, ever since I was a kid."

"Thank you for showing me, Nibbles, and sharing where your name came from. She is just the softest, sweetest thing." Aria giggled as, Nibbles wiggled her head up to rest against, Aria's neck.

Thumper laughed as he watched his rabbit steal, Aria's heart. It was just what she had needed. He mentally patted himself on the back. "Well you wouldn't think she was so sweet if she were under the covers with you, and decided to nibble on your toes." He laughed out loud.

Aria broke into laughter, joining in with, Thumper. He had such a light hearted way about him. Always happy and trying to make the best out of any situation. She liked that most of all about him.

Aria grabbed her head, her wolf howling. Something was wrong, it was a female in the natural wolf pack. She was in pain, unbearable pain

"Thumper, it's a female in the natural pack, she is whelping a liter of pups and she is in trouble. We have to go to her, she is in the cave. I didn't even know there was a female in the pack. Hurry, we have to go!"

She stood to begin removing her clothing. Thumper reached for her and then thought better of it, he didn't want his scent on her, Wraithe would kill him.

"Aria, we can't, it's late and it's too dangerous for you to be out there with just me to protect you. Wraithe would kill me if I let anything happen to you. Have you forgotten about that rogue wolf, what he did to those two males?"

She slowed from removing her clothes, and turned to stare at Thumper. A deep growl rolled up through her chest, she straightened herself, raising her chin in defiance.

"Thumper, you can stay or you can go, but I am going to that female. Do you understand?" Aria asked, her upper lip lifting up to show her canines that had already dropped from her gums.

This was not just, Aria, any longer, this was his alpha female and she had just commanded his obedience. In his head his wolf had already dropped his head and angled it to give access to his throat. Thumper didn't like it, but he began undressing.

In a matter of minutes they had both undressed and shifted. Aria used her teeth to grip the handle of the door, opening it, she jumped from the porch and headed toward the mountain. Thumper, and, Zeus, following behind her.

"Aria, Aria, what are you doing?" Wraithe asked across their link, fear clearly evident in his voice.

"There is a female wolf in the pack, she is whelping her pups and is in trouble. I have to go to her, Wraithe, and don't you dare tell me not to!"

"Love, please don't do this, it's not safe, and I'm too far away from you if you get in trouble."

"Wraithe, Thumper, and, Zeus are with me. I will cover our scents with the wind and hide our tracks. I swear I will be safe."

"I will come to you at the cave as soon as I can little love."

"Finish what you need to finish, Wraithe, I will see you soon." With that, Aria broke the link and picked up speed.

Chapter 20

'Damn it, what does she think she is doing, putting herself in danger.' Wraithe thought, as his beast took the head of one of the deputies. *"Little one is alpha female, she must do what is hers to do."* The beast replied, watching as the body finished turning to ash.

While, Wraithe looked on the most amazing thing happened, through the beasts' eyes he watched as a pale light raised from the ash, and soared into the sky. He somehow felt honored that he had witnessed such a thing. *"Spirit safe now."* The beast whispered.

Wraithe had never been much of a believer. Oh he had prayed when he was younger, but he must have done something wrong because there was never an answer to his prayers. *"Maybe no answer, was answer."* The beast said, as he turned and moved back into the shadows.

"Wraithe, Luna, is gone. We can't find her anywhere, we just overheard her grandmother calling the Sheriff. She should have been home a couple of hours ago." Reaper said across the link while walking up to, Wraithe, in his wolf form.

"Where was the last place you caught her scent?"

"The street, near the jail. She might be in there but the scent of those things is so strong on that part of street we can't tell if she is in there or if she has been taken back to that camp. The twins are watching the jail."

"How many are in the jail?"

"Four."

"Lets go."

∞

When they started out from the cabin it wasn't long before the wind brought the scent to them, they were being followed, by someone or some thing. She knew that scent, she had smelled it before, in the woods with the two dead wolves. Aria called to the wind, and hid their scents but she knew their tracks could be followed. She had to wait until they got to an area where the snow was deeper, then the wind could move it around to hide their tracks.

"Do you smell it, Thumper?"

"Yeah, we need to hurry."

∞

Wraithe, and the rest of his pack watched from the shadows, it was after midnight, but because of where the jail was located the risk of being seen by anyone in town if they went in was an obstacle. They needed a plan.

Luna knew she was in trouble, kinda hard to miss she thought. Hands cuffed behind her back, locked in a cell, tape covering her mouth, and the obscene things coming out of her captors mouths was scaring the hell out of her. The really large one, Mack she thought she heard them call him, he had said she belonged to their boss, and was not to be touched, but he had left an hour ago. Now it was being debated how their boss would even know if they had a little fun.

She could sense the wolves outside but how could they help her? She was trapped inside. Unci, her grandmother, had made her promise not to use her magic, but she was going to have to break that promise. Her captors would come for her soon and she wasn't about to allow them to use her body like that.

They were coming, she thought and at that moment the door opened and in walked three of them.

"Look at those tits, I bet her nipples are pointed and pink, just waiting to be sucked." The larger of the men said, licking his lips like she was steak or something.

"Yeah, well I have an idea for that sweet mouth of hers." One of the others replied, while he unlocked the cell door and pulled it open.

Luna starred at the three men, but it was the third that scared her the most. He had nothing to say, but the look in his eyes made her tremble. She backed into the corner doing her best to brace herself. Two of them lunged at her, each of them grasping an arm to pull her away from the wall. The third, the scary one walked up, and grabbed the top of her dress right between her breasts, and pulled. The heavy material split apart like it was nothing more than a paper bag.

She screamed but it was useless, the tape across her mouth muffled any sound. The men that had grabbed her arms each reached for a breast, and squeezed, the pain making her cry out again from behind her gag.

Please forgive me Unci. Luna closed her eyes, and concentrated on the earth around, and below the jail. She called to the great earth spirit to help her, to make the ground tremble, and shake.

In only moments the walls began to shake, dust falling from the ceiling, the ground trembling beneath them. The window in the cell wall began to rattle, it groaned against the weight of the wall around it.

The men stepped away from her, looking around as they braced themselves. One of them said 'earthquake', Luna wasn't sure which one. She had to concentrate on calling the earth.

The glass in the window shattered, but the bars remained. Metal came from the earth but after it was manipulated into a form it was harder to control, and if it was iron she would not be able to use her magic at all.

As Luna stared at the metal asking it to pull from the wall she saw two large hands grasp the bars, and pull. The three men in the cell grabbed her trying to pull her back, and out through the cell door. It was at that moment that three very large wolves snarled at her attackers from the hallway. They released her to take a fighting stance just as the bars were pulled from the window.

Luna rushed to the cot, climbing on top she stuck her head, and the tops of her shoulders out the window. She tried her best to wiggle further out, but once her feet left the cot she had no leverage. Concentrating on the metal cuffs to open, and release her she was startled when large hands grasped her from the outside, and began to pull her through.

She couldn't help the shriek of pain that lanced through her as her bare front scraped against the cement of the window opening. Even with the shriek being muffled by the tape her rescuer had heard her, he slowed his pull on her. Reaching for the tape he quickly pulled it from her mouth, she gasped, and closed her eyes doing her best not to scream. Wetness from her tears coating her dark lashes.

The metal of the cuffs broke open, finally her hands were free, and she pulled them around her to lift herself as much as she could in the opening. Her rescuer moved forward placing her arms on his shoulders he reached in to grasp her sides and lift her before he once again moved backwards, pulling her from the opening, and setting her on the ground before moving away.

Relief flooded through, Luna, and so did the adrenaline, easing some of the pain from the scrapes that ran from just above her breasts down to her abdomen. She realized her dress was still open all the way down and quickly she grasped both sides, pulling them together tightly. She looked up into the face of the man who had saved her. He had shoulder length black hair, and golden eyes that looked back at her so kindly.

"Thank you."

"No problem, my name is Wraithe, we need to get you out of here. I know you are hurt but we have to get you safe before we can take care of those cuts. Can you walk or do you need me to carry you?"

"I can walk, and I don't live far from here. I will go there now. Thank you again."

"Luna, that's your name, right, Luna?" Wraithe watched as she nodded her head up and down. "Luna, look your still in danger, if you go home they will just come there for you. My pa... my team live in the woods not far from here. You can stay with me, and my wife until we can work this out, alright?"

"That is very kind, but my grandmother, I can't leave her, she will be all alone."

While, Wraithe was thinking about that, the twins pulled up in the SUV.

"Listen, Luna, go with the twins. They will take you to grab some things, and get your grandmother. It's not safe, do you understand, you need to get her, and stay with us for a little while. Okay?"

He was right, Luna knew that he was. She turned, walking to the SUV, Hawk jumping from the passenger seat to open the back door and help her in.

"Take her home, and help her get her grandmother, then take them to my cabin. She is cut up pretty bad so be easy with her, but quick." Hawk gave a slight nod, and got back into the SUV. Wraithe watched as they pulled out quickly.

Wraithe ran to the front of the jail, walking in he saw his pack standing over the three piles of ash. He also looked around at the damage that had been done on the inside of the jail. His beast spoke up. *"Young one is gift, another warrior will come."* "She did this?" Wraithe asked his beast even though he already knew the answer. There was only one of his pack that hadn't met, Luna. He rubbed his face, and wondered how that was going to go.

Chapter 21

Aria sighed in relief as the last pup left its mother's body, and was placed in front of the mother wolf for her to clean. She was tired, and weak, but Aria felt she would be okay now. It was the first pup that had caused all the problems, it was turned, a breech. Aria didn't know the first thing about helping an animal deliver its young, but she did know that the pup had to be turned. There was nothing to do, but try, and do it herself. It helped that she had such small hands.

The female wolf was older, and this would be her last liter, she had been the alpha female of this pack, but her mate had died. The young male wolf that had taken over the pack was from her first liter. It was late in the year for pups to be born, but it seemed the mother wolf kept stopping herself from having the pups because they had so recently been transplanted here. That was at least what Aria felt she understood from her wolf.

This cave would be safe, and offered plenty of shelter for the new pups. Aria smiled as she watched them wiggle, and push to get to their mother to eat. One thing she did know was that new wolf pups were blind, and deaf at birth, they would remain that way for a while but she wasn't sure how long.

They were so beautiful, and, Aria had such a feeling of contentment as she watched the new mother with her liter. There were four of them so it wouldn't be long before the female would have her hands full. Aria giggled, oops, it's paws, not hands, she thought to herself.

"Aria, we need to get back." Thumper said, stepping close to look at the pups.

"Yeah, your right, we need to get back." She said, before yawning.

She was lucky when they had arrived that she had clothes to put on. Thankfully, Wraithe had thought to have some of her clothes brought here when they were stocking the cave. While she moved over to the corner, and began removing her clothes so she could shift, Thumper had gone outside to wait. Folding her clothes, and putting them away, she shifted.

Turning back to look at the pups she wandered back over, licking each one before she nuzzled the face of the mother, and then moved to the entrance of the cave to leave.

Thumper met her there, and once again they were loping through the forest and heading home. Aria was exhausted, it must be almost dawn, all she could think about was getting back home to her bed, and hopefully her mate.

"Wraithe?" Aria called across their link.

"My love, are you alright?"

"Yeah, just tired. We are on our way back home. Oh, Wraithe, wait till you see the new pups, they are so sweet."

Wraithe could feel how tired she was, it was like a living thing beating across their link. He gave her a brief explanation of what had happened, warning her of the guests she would find at the cabin.

"I won't be long, little love, get some rest. Aria, be safe."

"I will be handsome, hurry home."

Aria, and, Thumper, picked up speed moving through the forest as quickly as they could. She was so tired that all she could concentrate on was keeping pace with Thumper. They had just reached the edge of the clearing when a deep growl broke into the silence.

Thumper stopped, turning quickly to face the threat behind them. Aria stood at, Thumper's flank, and stared in surprise as another beast stepped from the trees. It was the same smell from the forest, the rogue wolf only this wasn't just a wolf, this was one of the warrior wolves. He smelled bad, and Aria's wolf sneezed before she too growled back at the beast before them.

"Aria, run!" She heard, Wraithe scream in her head.

"I can't, Wraithe, I can't leave, Thumper." She cried across their link.

The beast growled again as it began slowly moving around them, sizing them up for a meal is what went through, Aria's mind. Aria moved as, Thumper did, never taking their eyes off the threat. Her wolf snarling, and growling just as Thumper's did.

Growls came from across the clearing, the twins, they were coming. The beast growled again as it stared at the approaching wolves. "You think they can stop me, I'm stronger, and faster." Aria could swear she heard it laugh.

The twins moved in slowly once they reached, Aria, and, Thumper. Between the three they formed a line in front of her. "Go, Aria." Snow spoke quietly, his words barely having reached her mind before all hell broke loose.

The beast moved in quickly swiping at all three, its great claws barely missing their mark. Then it happened, in no more than seconds, Thumper rose, a great black beast standing there in his place, quickly pulling his sword from its sheath. The twins moved back, pushing, Aria further from the fray as they did.

Thumper swung the sword at the beast, nicking him in the side as he jumped back, just barely missing the cut that would surely have gutted him. Grabbing at his side he quickly turned, taking off into the forest.

Aria stared at, Thumper, his great head raising to the sky as he howled in his anger. Lowering his head he turned to stare back at, Aria, and the twins. He began to pull great breaths of air into his lungs. "Mate." Aria heard him say before he started moving toward the cabin. Aria could hear the soft purr he made as he passed her. She scented the air as well, Luna, she thought.

"Thumper, wait, Thumper, stop!" Aria shouted across the link. The beast halted, and turned to stare at her. He bowed his head, and put his great fist to his chest. "My alpha." The beast whispered.

Aria spoke softly as she walked up to stand in front of the beast, still in her own wolf form. He lowered to one knee before her. "Warrior, your mate is young, she does not know you yet or your ways. If you go to her this way, you will frighten her, do you understand? She needs to know the man first."

The beast let out a heavy sigh before nodding at Aria. As she watched, Thumper, the man, took the beasts place. Aria leaned forward and licked, Thumper's cheek. "Welcome back." She whispered across the link.

"They are beautiful wolves." A soft voice said, coming from the direction of the tree line.

The three wolves turned to stare at the young woman standing there along the tree line. They hadn't heard her approach or even scented her for that matter.

Thumper stood quickly and stared at the young woman, thank the heavens he was dressed. Her hair was as black as a raven and hung long and straight all the way to the tops of her thighs. But it was her eyes that caught his attention the most. Blue, they were the blue of a bright clear sky in the light of day. Her skin pale like moonlight. His wolf yelped in his head. His beast purred. *"Mate, our mate."*

"Yeah, they are." He replied, not really sure what else to say. "You must be, Luna, Wraithe called and said to expect you. I'm Thumper. It's pretty cold out here, why don't we head back to the cabins."

Aria, and, the twins quickly darted off, heading back into the forest. Thumper walking toward Luna and gently taking her hand to pull her back toward, Wraithe's cabin.

Thumper, what an odd name, Luna thought. It was probably a nickname, but, Thumper, she wondered how he had gotten it.

Chapter 22

Wraithe stormed into the cabin, he had barely remembered to change back from the beasts' form. He needed his mate, and he needed her now, she had disobeyed him, she had risked her life. What if she had been killed, his blood turned cold. There would be no hole, no hell that could hide the monster from him that would dare take her.

She was coming down the hall, and still he could feel the exhaustion that was all over her, but he could not calm himself. Reaching her he lifted her into his arms getting a startled yelp from her as he headed to their room.

Looking back over his shoulder he saw the awkward looks from his guests, and, Thumper. Sending a quick 'deal with it' over his link to, Thumper, Wraithe continued on his way. Before closing the door he heard, Thumper laugh as he said. "Newlyweds."

"Wraithe? What's wrong?"

He let her legs lower, pulling her closer as he did. Wraithe buried his face in the hair at her neck, moving it away to find his mark. He licked it, coaxing a small moan from his female. Wraithe couldn't contain the deep growl that rumbled up from his chest, feeling his mate tense at the sound.

"You disobeyed me." He said, while moving to sit her on the bed before he knelt in front of her.

"Wraithe, I couldn't leave, Thumper, alone to face that thing."

"Aria, Thumper is a seasoned soldier, he can take care of himself. When I told you to run from that monster, I meant it. You should have done what you were told!" He said, another growl passing over his lips.

"What I was told? Who do you think you are that you can order me to do anything?" Her own growl adding more strength to her words. Aria gripped the quilt with her fingers, as she suddenly felt the fear, not anger, pure fear coming from her mate. The tension in her muscles leaving her immediately. Oh, God, what had she done, she asked herself.

Aria raised her hand, and gently placed it on, Wraithe's cheek. "It's okay, my love, I'm okay and I'm so very sorry." She looked into his eyes, tears filling her own.

Wraithe leaned forward, and lowered his head to rest in her lap. Her hands moved to push the long black hair from his face, offering the comfort she knew he needed.

"Don't ever do it again, Aria. I thought I would lose you, and I could not get to you fast enough, even with the speed of the beast I couldn't get to you. Everything between us has happened so quickly. Until now we haven't even had an argument. And none of that matters, there is not a part of my body that you do not reside in. I cannot lose you, Aria, do you hear me, I cannot lose you." Wraithe raised his head to stare into her eyes, his own watering from the emotion that rode him so hard. He had never felt anything like this love he had for her, and he would risk everything to keep it.

Aria sat silently listening to her mate, feeling the love for her pouring from him. Slipping forward she wrapped her legs around his waist, her arms wrapping around his strong shoulders. With all of her being she sent comfort and love back to her mate, gently resting her head against his beating heart while she pulled him tighter against her.

"I love you, Wraithe, with all that I am, I love you. I know what has happened between us was fast. We still have so much to learn about each other, but from the first moment that you wrapped your arms around me, I have known that we were meant to be. We were two halves that are now one whole. I think that whatever is out there, that brought us together, knew that it must be this way between us, so that we could face what is coming. We will, face it together, Wraithe, and you will not lose me. I trust in you to always protect me, and when you are not with me, then the pack will be. Trust me to know that is the way it has to be."

Aria pulled from, Wraithe, just enough to raise her lips to meet his. He immediately opened to her, darting his tongue in to play with hers. There was no frenzy in this kiss, no urgent passion, like what was normal in their lovemaking. No, tonight was for loving, for soft touches, and deep caresses. Tonight was a night for their souls, and it was their souls that reached out to touch, to wrap themselves in each other so tightly that they could never be separated again.

∞

As the fog of sleep began lifting from, Wraithe he noticed one thing, his mate was not beside him. He reached for her across their link and was immediately hit by worry. Wraithe quickly left his bed and pulled on a pair of jeans, reaching for the door as he zipped them, and stepped into the hall.

"Aria?" He called, making his way to the front of the cabin. He found her pacing in front of the large windows. Her arms wrapped tightly around her middle. Reaching for her, he pulled her into his arms. "What's wrong, my love?"

"Oh, Wraithe." She cried, burying her face in his chest. "Zeus, I can't find, Zeus. The pups, he went with us to deliver the pups yesterday. I was so tired, Wraithe, I wasn't thinking. I must have left him there, oh, God, Wraithe, you don't think he tried to follow me home, not with that monster out there?"

Wraithe looked around, making sure their guests were not within hearing distance. "Aria, did you call to the natural pack?"

"Yes, but they haven't answered me, Wraithe, well not exactly."

"What do you mean, not exactly?"

"I think they were hunting. What I get from my wolf is that something disturbed them this morning, now they are chasing it. Wait, Wraithe, what if it's that monster?"

Wraithe called to the pack, his wolf much stronger than, Arias', and would be able to understand more. They had been hunting something, it had gotten too close to the den. Through his wolf he could smell what they were after, it was the other beast. Shit! He thought to himself. They were circling back toward the den now.

"Aria, they were chasing that rogue, I'm going to head up there, make sure they are safe, and find, Zeus. You stay here, do you understand? I can't help them if I'm worried about you. Please, promise me. Besides, Zeus might come back, and you don't want him to follow your scent back out again, do you?"

"No, I don't. Okay, I will stay here, but please, Wraithe, be careful."

Wraithe leaned down and placed a quick kiss on her lips. "I promise, love."

He turned quickly and headed for the front door. Opening his link with his own pack he confirmed they were out on the morning perimeter run. "Doc, Thumper, the two of you move back in close to the cabin, keep an eye on our guests, and Aria." Where were his guests by the way, he wondered.

"They are here in the rec room, Wraithe, watching some TV." Aria spoke across their link."

"Good, keep them inside, my love. See you soon."

∞

While Blackie made his way back around toward the cave he replayed the conversation from earlier this morning.

"So she is his mate, how the hell did that happen?"

"Apparently your demons aren't the only forces at work. We all will get mates, and when we do, that will trigger our larger wolves to make an appearance."

Blackie slammed his fist down on the hood of the truck, denting the metal. So much for his plans to get one over on, Wraithe, to have the bigger and better wolf. "Damn!" He said, holding back the scream of rage that was boiling in him.

"At least you have the demons, I don't want a fucking mate. You know how I feel about women!"

"Maybe your mate will be a guy."

"No, not possible, these women are all witches, given their powers by some ancient Goddess. Aria controls the air."

"And I'm just hearing about this now, because?"

"There has been too much going on. I couldn't get away before now." He spoke as he turned back to face Blackie. The only man on the team who knew his secret.

Blackie walked up to his former team member, grabbing him he whirled him around to face the truck, whispering in his ear. "Yeah, well be both know why you really came, now don't we? Now turn around and get on your knees."

Blackie shook his head to clear his thoughts, not a good time to be walking down memory lane. For now he had lost the natural wolves, and this was as good a spot as any to wait. He dug his claws into the tree, scaling it quickly to find a lower branch that would support his weight.

∞

Aria stepped out onto the porch but went no further. She needed to do something to help, Wraithe. "Old friend, come to me." She called, smiling as the slight breeze wrapped around her, lifting her hair.

"Go to, Wraithe, and the others, cover their scents and tracks." Aria turned to go back inside, but came face to face with Luna.

"You use your magic?" Luna asked, excitement shining clearly in her bright blue eyes.

Aria smiled at the wide eyed young woman, and decided it was time to get to know one another. "Yes, Luna, I did use my magic, and very soon you will be using yours as well. What is your magic by the way?"

"I speak for the earth." Luna responded, lowering her head slightly as though she were ashamed, that, or she was preparing to be ridiculed.

Aria stepped forward, and raised her hand to place a finger below, Luna's chin, raising it to look into the young woman's eyes.

"Do not be ashamed or afraid here, Luna. There are things happening now that are frightening in our world. Here you are protected, and will be encouraged to use your gift."

"My Unci, my grandmother, has warned me that it will not be understood, and that I should not use it. She made me promise, but I will explain it to her."

"You do not have to explain, child, it is time."

Both women turned quickly to face the older woman now standing with them on the porch.

Aria was surprised that even her wolf had not heard the old woman. "You have the gift as well, don't you?" She asked.

"Yes, each generation of the women in my family are born with the gift from the great mother."

"But, Unci, why didn't you tell me? What is it that is coming?"

"Ah, child, it isn't coming, it is here. A great evil walks the earth now, and it will only spread. Now your training will begin."

Unci moved down the stairs and waved to, Aria, and, Luna, to join her.

Chapter 23

Wraithe moved through the forest heading for the cave as quickly as he could while scenting the air for the monster. He had called to the natural pack, and told them to return to the cave. Warning them of danger, he knew it was out there, his beast knew it too, but where? The scent was coming from every direction, and, Wraithe felt like he was inside a giant circle. And wouldn't you just know that the cave was right smack in the middle.

He was almost at the cave when he stopped to look around, he didn't want to lead that monster anywhere near the entrance. He noticed his prints in the snow were now covered, a slight breeze lifting his fur. Aria, he thought as he raised his muzzle to the air, and took a deep breath. He could still scent the monster, but his own scent was gone.

Blackie had spotted, Wraithe, just as he began moving away from the area. He hadn't found the entrance to the cave, but he had made sure to leave his scent around the entire place. For now his plan seemed to be working, Wraithe was scenting the air, but didn't seem to be able to pinpoint a direction.

He picked up speed when he felt he was out of hearing distance, time to head for his true target.

Wraithe entered the cave, letting his eyes adjust to the darkness, and shifting back to his normal form. He finally spotted what he was looking for. Curled up over in the corner was, Zeus. He lifted his head when he spotted, Wraithe, and wagged his long heavy tail, but he didn't get up, and come to him.

Wraithe walked over to the big dog, concerned he was injured, and knelt down. Snuggled against, Zeus, were four sleeping pups. They were all wrapped up tight against the lab, buried in his fur for warmth. Wraithe smiled, and shook his head. "Now what have you gotten yourself into, babysitting?"

The big lab whined, and then looked away toward another wall of the cave. Wraithe stood, and walked over to the mother wolf. He knelt beside her, rubbing his hand down along her soft fur, she was gone. The birth of the pups must have been too much for her. The young alpha male, Wraithe had fought, sat to the side. He moved forward to nudge the head of the female, then sat and stared into, Wraithe's eyes. "I'm sorry." Wraithe said, and then stood to go build the fire that would carry her home.

∞

The women entered the cabin laughing. It had been a wonderful morning, each of them playing with their magic, and showing off just a little as well. Aria had taught, Luna, to use her hands when she called her magic, just as the warrior had taught her. Luna's eyes becoming even brighter with the excitement when her requests of the earth were performed. Her magic was very strong, and, Aria felt a sense of pride in the young woman.

Aria grasped her chest, tears falling from her eyes. The female wolf had died, and, Wraithe was building the fire. He would be bringing the pups' home, there wasn't another female in the pack, and without their mother, they would not survive.

Aria remembered her guests, and looked up quickly, they both were crying quietly. Aria hadn't explained about the wolves, so how could they know what had happened? "How did you know?"

"Wolves are of the earth, the earth has told us of the loss." Luna said, softly, reaching to her grandmother, and clasping her hand. "Her pups will die."

"No, I won't allow it." Aria said firmly. "Wraithe, and I, are tied to that pack, he is bringing the pups' home to me. I helped deliver them last night, and I was so tired I left my lab, Zeus, at the den. Wraithe went to get him, and found the mother."

"How do you know all this, Aria, I didn't see you on a phone."

Aria looked at, Luna, then smiled. "Yeah, well about that, have you ever heard of shifters?"

"Aria, it's here!" Thumper screamed across their link.

Before, Aria could even move, the side door burst open, slamming against the wall. Standing in the doorway was the monster. Blood dripping from his claws.

Without another thought, Aria shifted, her wolf moving to stand in front of the two women who now huddled on the floor by the sofa. Aria raised her paw, snarling back at the monster. The wind grew as she watched, and she could see the fur on the monster being pulled back out of the door. He braced his great hands against the door frame, his long claws digging into the panels of wood around the door.

From behind him, Blackie felt the claws sink into his back, and side. It couldn't be, not Wraithe, he was still up on the mountain. Snarling he released his hold on the door allowing the wind to take him. It had the desired effect, pulling him back hard against the new beast. They fell together down the steps, rolling onto the ground outside the cabin. Blackie jumped quickly to his feet, ignoring the pain from his wounds.

The other beast was just as fast, coming to his feet, pulling the sword from its sheath on his back.

Inside, Aria, licked, Luna's face, and whined. Then she moved, chuffing at the two women to follow her. They must have understood what she wanted because they climbed to their feet, and followed her. Aria ran to the pantry, locking her teeth around the handle she opened the door. Walking inside, Aria found the panel hidden on the wall of a shelf, using her paw she scratched at it. The shelf began to move, pushing forward, and then turning slightly after clearing the rest of the shelves.

Aria backed up, and stared at the women, then chuffed. Again they knew what she was trying to tell them, and moved into the darkness beside the shelf. The movement inside triggered the sensor and a pale light lit the inside. Seeing the steps the two began to follow them down. Aria once more scratched at the panel, and the shelves began to shift back into place. Turning she ran to the side door leaving the cabin.

Thumper, and, Blackie, circled each other, but each time, Thumper struck out with the sword, Blackie was able to maneuver out of the way. While the two fought, Thumper noticed other men, ones carrying the demons begin to move in from the trees.

"Wraithe?" Aria called, across the link.

"I know, my love, I'm almost there."

One of the demons stepped onto the porch from the steps at the front of the cabin. His foot no sooner hit the step then he was being pulled from the porch by Luca, who delivered a swift punch to the face that sent the man the rest of the way down. Reaper was already fighting against two of the others.

Aria caught another scent of blood, Doc, she thought. Moving quickly, but as silently as possible so she didn't draw any notice, she moved down the steps. Laying in the dirt was Doc, his throat slashed, but he was still alive. Aria nudged his head, his eyes opening to stare at her. "Doc, can you hear me? Can you get inside the cabin?" Aria asked, across the link.

"No."

He hadn't had a chance to shift so luckily he was still wearing clothes. With her head, Aria moved his head to the side, biting into the collar of his shirt she began to pull. He was really heavy she thought to herself, but her wolf only chuffed back at her. She was strong, she could do this. Once she had finally gained enough ground that she was able to pull him easier, Aria worked her way under the porch. Leaving, Doc, hidden behind the shrubs, and snow.

Another man was about to sneak up on, Luca, when, Aria got back to the porch. She raised her paw, and then brought it down hard against the porch. While she watched the wind picked up the man, and threw him against a tree. Startled, Luca looked at the man, then up to the porch, and, Aria, giving a quick nod to her, he reengaged in the fighting.

Coming out of nowhere another man jumped onto, Thumper's back, causing him to whirl in another direction. At that moment, Aria heard an all too familiar growl, Wraithe, she thought, and she and her wolf chuffed.

With one swipe of, Wraithe's claws he sent the man on, Thumper's back flailing into the air, landing right at, Reaper's feet. Reaper swung his great sword severing the head from the shoulders as quick as that. Leaving, Wraithe to face the monster.

Wraithe didn't have his sword which meant the battle with the monster would be more physical blows, and swipes of claws. Throwing themselves at each other, grabbing, and slashing with their claws, Wraithe finding an opening to bury his huge fangs into his opponent. The monster howled at the pain, digging his claws into, Wraithe's side.

Aria didn't have a clue when the twins had arrived, but, Wraithe was right, they were deadly. As she watched, the battle in the yard was all but over as she watched one head after another roll from its body. The last two fighters, Wraithe, and the monster.

Again he found the opening to strike at the neck of the monster, only this time when he pulled back flesh came with his fangs. Blood spurting from the wound, it fell to its knees.

Wraithe stepped back to take a sword from, Reaper, his only thought was to remove the head.

No one but, Aria, saw the red dot that marked, Wraithe's heart. Before her scream could leave her throat she watched him fall.

Shifting as she ran, Aria fell to her knees at his side. "Wraithe!" She screamed at him. "God, no, please no. Wraithe!"

Wraithe opened his eyes to stare into the beautiful green eyes of his mate. He felt no pain, except the pain caused by her tears. He coughed roughly. "My love, please don't cry."

"No, Wraithe, don't you dare leave me, don't you dare! You promised me, you promised me a lifetime."

"I, I love you, little one." He closed his eyes, and, Aria screamed.

Chapter 24

Doc had been moved inside, thankfully the slash to his throat had not reached his carotid. A few stitches were all that marked where the slash had been. With their quick healing he would be fine in a matter of hours.

Hawk had gone for, Zeus, and the pups', he had found them safe and unharmed. They were now on their way back to the cabin.

Thumper opened the door to the underground den. He owed, Aria, everything for saving his mate. As he, and the two women stepped from the pantry, Wraithe's body was being brought into the cabin. Thumper could not stop the tears that fell from his eyes. Death was a constant companion in their line of work, but this time there was nothing to console him. As he watched, he felt a gentle pressure on his hand. Luna, had placed her hand in his, entwining their fingers. Although he wanted to howl at the pleasure of her touch, he couldn't. The weight on his heart was just too heavy.

Aria held herself straight and tall as she walked beside her fallen mate. Her love. She wanted him placed in their mated bed where she could wash his body and say her goodbyes in the privacy of their room.

She had stood in front of, Reaper, and asked that a large pyre be built for her mate. They would send him home tonight. "Aria, wouldn't you rather we buried him, for you, a grave nearby?" Aria had smiled, and placed her hand on, Reaper's heart. "No, Reaper, but thank you. Please build the pyre, it is the way of the warrior, and we will send him home that way." She had turned before seeing the tears that fell from Reapers' lowered chin.

Alone in their room, Aria, had taken her time to wash the blood and dirt from her mate's body. Heavy tears falling to his skin. Caressing every inch, and committing it to memory.

A soft knock came at the door, and, Aria walked slowly to take the cloth from, Luca, that she had asked for. Smiling softly she had given her thanks before turning back to her mate.

She had no clue why this particular cloth, and color be used, only that it was what must drape her mate. The velvet was so soft, and luxurious to the touch, the deep crimson a shade she had always admired. Spreading the cloth she admired the richness of it. It was all that would do for her mate. She prayed that it kept him wrapped with love in the heavens, until she could wrap her arms around him again.

As she spread the cloth slowly up his body she wondered how she would go on. When she reached his face she leaned in slowly to place one last kiss upon his lips. "I will follow when I can my love." Then lightly she let the cloth fall to cover his face.

Pulling a black sweater over her head, she moved to the door, and opened it. Standing in the hall she looked to the faces of her pack. Each stood lining the hallway dressed in black shirts, and jeans. Their swords strapped to their backs. Turning in the quick fluid movement as one, marking them as the warriors they were, they each took a knee before her. Aria watched as they placed their fists upon their chests, and bowed their heads.

"He is ready to go home now." She said, quietly before stepping back, and into the room.

"Reaper, were the torches placed in the corners around the pyre, north, south, east, and west?"

"Yes, Aria, it was done."

Nodding, Aria stepped away to watch as her mate was lifted from their bed.

The stars were shining brightly tonight, Aria, thought. She had asked the wind to clear the clouds so it would be so. They were waiting to welcome him.

Aria had walked beside her mate as he was carried to this place. He had promised that beside her is where he would always be, and she would do no less for him even now. She was the mate of the Alpha, and she would walk with pride to honor him.

A great screech was heard over head as, Wraithe was lowered to the ground before he was to be lifted to the top of the pyre.

Gliding down from the sky was the largest white owl, Aria had ever seen. Almost to the ground its great wings pulled back to gracefully flap in the air, slowing its inward flight, but before it could reach the ground its form changed to that of a man. He stepped easily to the earth, not even the slightest sound announcing his steps. There in front of them stood the largest of men, golden in skin, and hair.

Walking to her the man bowed, then raised, and spoke. "Lady Aria, I am Wulfgar. First Warrior to Odin."

Aria didn't have any idea what to say. All she could do was stare at the man, and heaven help her, were those fangs she saw in his mouth? Hearing growls from her pack, Aria raised her arm. "Wait." Spoken so softly but she knew they heard her.

"Lady Aria, I mean no harm. I'm here to help. Your mate, he is not gone."

Aria let out a growl so vicious it surprised even her. "What do you mean he isn't gone? Please, do not do this, do not give me hope where there is none."

"He sleeps a healing sleep, that is all. His heart beat so slow it cannot be heard, even with your wolf hearing."

Aria rushed to, Wraithe's body, sliding to the ground, and pulling the cloth from his face.

"When will he wake? What can I do?"

Wulfgar moved to the opposite side of, Wraithe, then looked to, Aria. "There is nothing you can do, but I can speed things up a bit."

Raising his wrist to his lips he bit deeply then moved his wrist for the blood to drip to Wraithe's mouth.

Aria gasped. "What are you doing?"

"I am Vampire, my blood will speed his healing. He will wake soon." He said, pulling his wrist from, Wraithe's mouth, and then licking it to seal the wound.

"How can this be happening?" Aria asked, watching the face of her mate.

"I will explain further when he wakes. There, do you hear it now, his heart beats strong."

Aria listened, and there it was for all around them to hear. Her mate, she threw herself against him, tears pouring from her eyes while she clutched his body to hers.

"Wraithe, can you hear me, my love? I'm here, please, Wraithe, come back to me."

It was only a moment before, Aria felt strong arms wrap around her, and pull her close. She raised her head to stare into the most beautiful eyes in the world. Liquid amber, she thought.

"Did I miss something, little one, Aria, what is wrong?" He asked, concern clearly in his voice.

Loud guffaws, and laughing erupted around them. Backs were slapped, arms were thrown around each other. All of them watching with happiness at the return of their friend, and alpha.

Wraithe wasn't sure what was happening, why was everyone laughing? Why was his mate crying? What the fuck? He thought to himself. He started to move when a man's face he didn't know appeared above him. He just stood there over him with a smile on his face. Were those fangs? What the hell was going on?

Aria pulled from him, and stood. Reaching down she grabbed the hand he raised to her while he got to his feet. The cloth falling from him. Roars of laughter ripped through the people standing around him. "Enough!" Wraithe shouted.

Aria bent, and picked up the cloth, wrapping it around his waist.

"That should help, handsome." She said, unable to hold back her giggles any longer she joined in with the rest.

Chapter 25

They had all gone back to the cabin, Wraithe still fuming over finding out that the monster's body hadn't been found. That meant there was a real possibility it was still out there alive. Worse was the thought that the damn thing would come again for, Aria.

The stranger, Wulfgar, was now standing with them while lots of liquor was being passed around to celebrate, Wraithe's return. He was still in shock over that, but the stranger had promised answers, and, Wraithe's temper was beginning to raise at the delay in getting those answers. He had put on clothes, and like everyone else stood waiting.

Aria moved to his side, and as he wrapped his arm around her to pull her in close, Wulfgar stepped in front of him. The room grew silent as the man began to speak.

"The Order of the Blood Wolf is now born. Wraithe, when you, and your mate blood bonded immortality for you, and your mate came into being. It was a promise made long ago by, Odin, to the Warrior Wolf that now walks with you. They were brave, and fought valiantly for this cause hundreds of years ago, but when the war of that time was over, the Blood Wolf was near extinction. Odin promised the mightiest of those wolves, yours, that should they be born again, immortality would be theirs, in honor of those that had fought so hard before them."

Wulfgar looked around the room, staring into the faces of all. "May I borrow your sword, and, Aria, please if you would gather the cloth that was used to cover your mate?" He asked while turning back to face them.

When the items were gathered and given to, Wulfgar, he turned once again to face, Wraithe, and, Aria. "Wraithe, if you would kneel, please." Doing as he had been asked, Wraithe lowered to one knee.

Wulfgar raised the rich crimson velvet and with a wave of his arm it was trimmed in long silver fur. He moved to drape the robe around, Wraithe's shoulders. Stepping back he then picked up Wraithe's sword, and laid it to rest against the deep red cloth on Wraithe's shoulder.

"Wraithe from this moment on, and into forever you are marked as King of the Lycan. May your line be mighty, and walk with honor, now and forevermore. Rise, King Wraithe."

Rising shakily to his feet, Wraithe looked around the room, staring at the shocked eyes of his pack. He had no idea what to say or even if he could believe what had just happened. There was a stinging in the center of his back between his shoulder blades, and he reached around to rub it.

Aria, shrieked, grabbing her chest. "Aria, what is wrong?" Wraithe, looked to Wulfgar. "What have you done, what is wrong with her?"

Wulfgar smiled, flashing those sharp white fangs, then lifted his shoulders, and shrugged. "Every King must have a Queen, she is now marked as Queen of the Lycan."

Aria pulled the neck of her sweater down, and looked at her chest. A beautiful tattoo of a vivid black wolf now rested against the top of her left breast. It wasn't large, and overwhelming, it fit perfectly, just above her heart. But then, what the hell, did it just move? Aria jerked her head a little further back to look closer at the wolf. His head now looking upward, golden eyes staring back at her.

"Wulfgar, what is this?" Aria asked, she knew how funny she must have looked in that moment. Her eyes felt like they were bugging out of their sockets.

Wulfgar laughed, and replied. "As king, there will be times that, Wraithe cannot come to you. A queen must always be protected so in times of need you only need to touch the wolf, and call to it. The wolf will leave your skin, and become real."

Aria looked back down at the wolf that now sat panting on her chest. "I need a drink."

Roars of laughter went up around the room. Wraithe moved closer to wrap his arms around her waist, he looked down at the wolf that now painted the skin on his mate's chest. "You behave yourself." He said, growling at the wolf, watching as it laid down and rested its head on its paws. Satisfied that the wolf now knew his place, Wraithe smiled brightly at his mate.

"Wraithe?"

Wraithe turned to look at, Wulfgar.

Again the man waived his arm, and, Aria's sweater, and jeans were replaced with a beautiful long gown. Rich layers of blood red gossamer now covered her from top to bottom. The top braided with dark rubies entwined within. Draping her shoulders, and running the length of her body was a beautiful silver, and white fur cape. The fur matching that of what trimmed, Wraithe's royal cape.

Wulfgar smiled, a well matched pair he thought. Leaning in for just Aria, and, Wraithe's ears, he spoke again. "We must step outside. You must be wed before the moon. Turning he began making his way to the side door. Aria, and, Wraithe following, with the pack right behind.

"Aria?" Wraithe asked. "Is this what you want, to be married to me?"

Aria turned a bright smiling face to her mate. "My love, we are already married as far as I'm concerned. I think this is just a formality, besides, look at us, we are already dressed for it." She said, giggling. She had her mate back, he wasn't gone, who cared about the rest.

Everyone walked quietly as they followed their alphas, once more in the clearing where they had almost burned, Wraithe. The pyre had already been lit, and burned brightly to light the night with a warm glow. Wulfgar stopped several feet from the blaze then turned to face the new King and Queen.

Aria, and, Wraithe took their places before the Vampire, waiting for what would come next. A long beautiful vine of white roses appeared in his hand. Wulfgar stepped to them, reaching for the left hand of each he raised them, and wrapped the vine around their wrists.

In a deep rich voice, Wulfgar, called upon the gods. "Lord Odin, Lady Earth, before you stand your children. We ask for your blessings as they unite under the moon. A mated pair, blessed by the moon and earth."

The air picked up to kiss the flame of the burning pyre, setting the blaze to burn higher and brighter. Large white flakes began to fall from the sky but as the flakes touched the ground murmurs rose, the flakes were not snow but white rose petals and the tips were a deep crimson.

Aria, and, Wraithe turned back to look at, Wulfgar. Questioning gazes clear on their faces.

"In the mountains of the Blood Wolves was a beautiful valley where these incredible white roses bloomed. The wolves believed the roses were a blessing from Lady Earth therefore matings, birth blessings, and deaths were performed among them. They were considered Holy, and became the symbol of the wolves. Their last battle was fought there, and by nightfall those roses were covered in blood. This is a blessing from Odin, a remembrance, and a promise. They will take root here, and will bloom year round."

"Wulfgar, thank you, for everything. The roses will be honored here as well." Aria said, turning to once again smile up into the face of her mate.

Wulfgar cleared his throat, and spoke again. "Turn to face your people please." He waited for them to turn then raised his voice once more. "May I present, King Wraithe, and, Queen Aria mated alphas of the Blood Wolves."

Whoops, and howls were raised all around. Luna, and, Unci making their way to the couple, the two bowed, and offered their congratulations. Aria stepped forward, and hugged them both close. "Well I guess the two of you know just about everything now." The three of them laughed, and pulled each other tight.

"Child, to have seen this in my lifetime is more than I could have asked for." Unci smiled, and hugged, Aria, once again.

"Excuse me, one last thing." Wulfgar spoke softly.

"The lycans will sense the rebirth of their king. They will begin to drift to you, bringing their mates and families. Train them well, every one of them will be needed. You will find when you check your finances that a very large sum of money has been deposited. It will help with your needs. With that being said, it's time for me to go. Be well King Wraithe, Queen Aria, be well."

With that the large vampire made his way off to the side just a bit, and as quickly as that, was once again the great white owl, exiting as quietly as he had arrived.

Hours later, Wraithe pulled his mate tighter against his chest. Raising his head to nuzzle into the soft tresses of her hair. God, how he loved her scent. She lay stretched out along the top of his body, and he couldn't remember a time when she hadn't been there. How perfectly her body fit in all the right places.

"Wraithe?"

"Yes, love?"

"It's not over, is it?"

"No, love. I'm afraid it's just the beginning."

Aria raised her head to stare into his golden eyes. "I love you, Wraithe, and come what may we will face it together as we are meant to."

Wraithe reached down and pulled her further up his body. Raising his head to press his lips against hers. He felt every ounce of the love she felt for him, and he gloried in the blessings that were his. He let go of the kiss, and lowered his head back down before he looked to the ceiling.

In his mind he spoke out into the heavens. "Thank you, may I honor you well for the blessings I have been given."

Clutching, Aria, he rolled her below him and licked his mark on her neck. The deep moan from his mate having a very nice effect on his lower body, he pressed it against her.

Laughing Aria chided him. "You are incorrigible." She said, reaching between them to grab his hardness.

Hi, thank you for reading Wolf's Song. I truly hope you enjoyed it. It's a dream come true. I would love to hear from you, so if you feel like it, please feel free to write to me.
Vickie82.brown@yahoo.com

Wolf's Moon, coming early 2015.

www.ingramcontent.com/pod-product-compliance
Lightning Source LLC
Chambersburg PA
CBHW070924130626
46555CB00001B/280